n

••

and I

dare to pursue my
authentic ambition

~~~~~~~~~~~~~~

Jenny Many
STRIKES GOLD

By Steve Hill

Jenny Many STRIKES GOLD

Published 2023

by Jenny Many Media Ltd

71-75 Shelton Street, Covent Garden, London, WC2H 9JQ, United Kingdom.

www.jennymany.com

Creative Director: Jay Canham

Book Publisher: Michael Brewer

ISBN: 978-1-7392499-0-8

Set in OpenDyslexic, an open source font created to increase readability for readers with dyslexia. https://opendyslexic.org/

Typeset by The Book Typesetters
www.thebooktypesetters.com

Printed and bound by CPI Group (UK) Ltd, Croydon, CR0 4YY

For Gill, Matty, Tom and Dad,
you've all made this possible.

Thank you to Jay, Steph, Mandy,
Andy, James, Stephen, Michael, TK,
Nic and Elspeth.

Dylan

Ella

@fluffadoodle

?

Lindy

Lily

Contents

#team TRIXIE

STAR Flakes

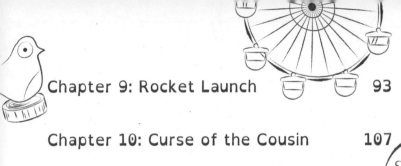

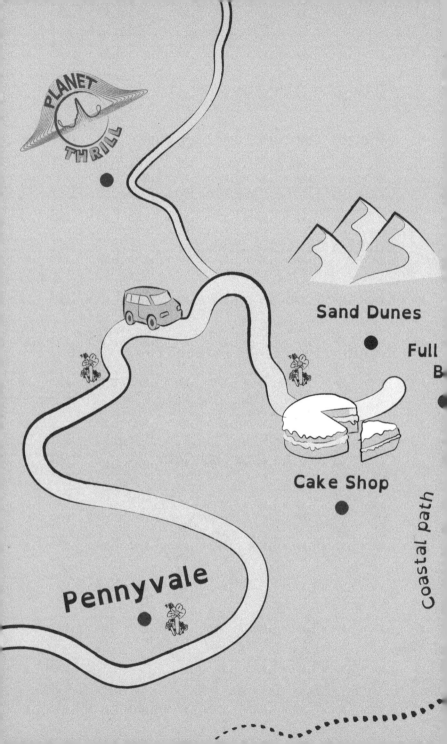

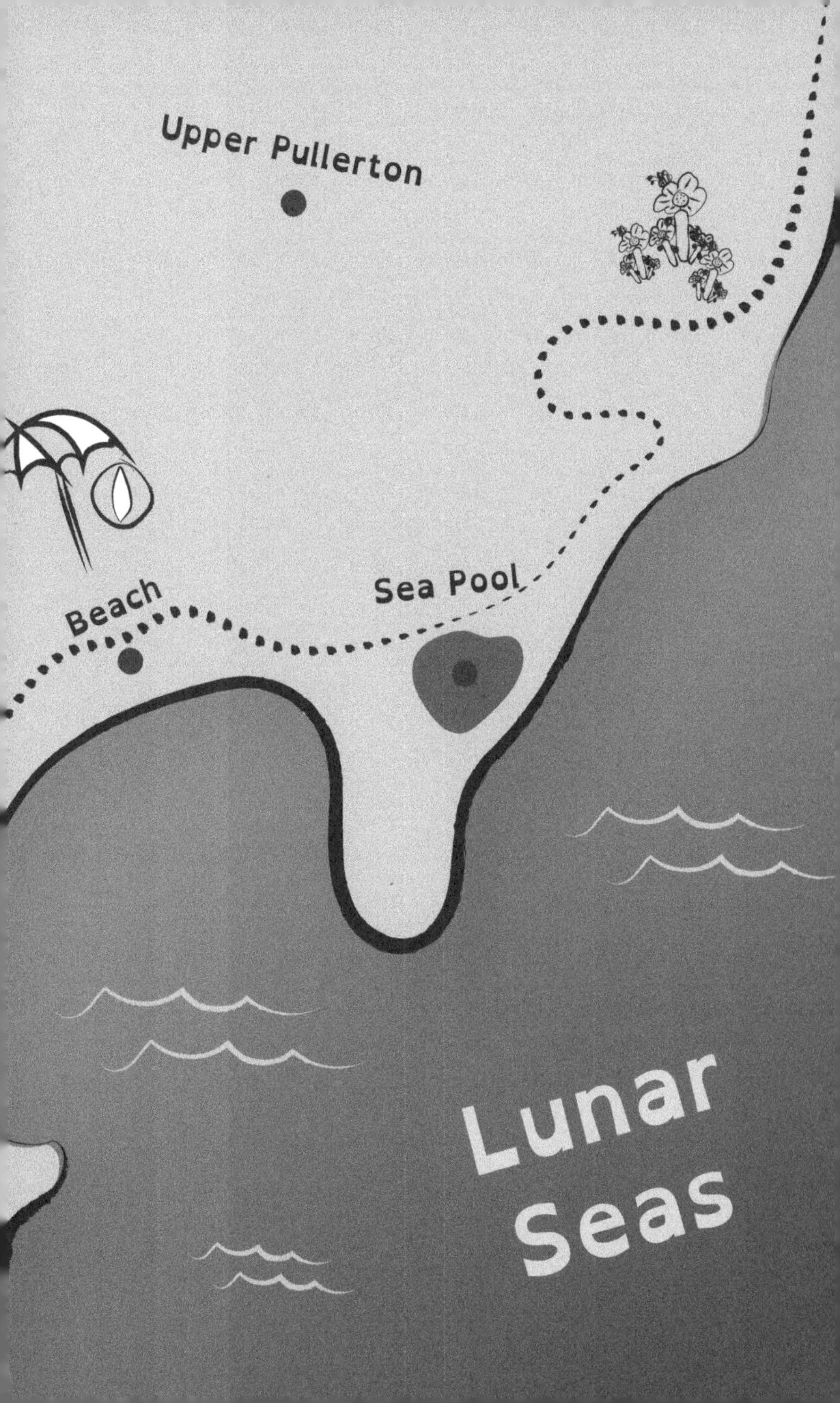

Upper Pullerton
Beach
Sea Pool
Lunar Seas

First Things First

Hi! My name is Jenny. Jenny Many. You may have heard of me, I'm kind of well known – in Pennyvale anyway. That's my town. If you haven't visited yet you should, we have a smoothie shack that makes the best mango mayhem juices, there's a skate park and cool shops like *Pete's Pets*. But the main reason I really love Pennyvale is because it's where my all friends live. I have the best friends. I mean I guess everyone says that about their friends, but mine REALLY are awesome.

Hannah Banerjee has been my BFF since ... forever. When I ask Mum exactly when me and Hannah first got close she says, 'you belly bonded'. That means we were friends before we were even born! Our mums met when they were expecting us and spent loads of time together doing pregnancy yoga and stuff like that. Mum says she obviously can't have got her relaxation right as I can't sit still for five minutes! Anyway, since me and Hannah came into the world we've done everything together. We even took our first steps at the same time. We were playing right here, in the living room of our house, when next door's cat came by and rubbed herself against the glass doors to the garden. All of a sudden we stopped crawling around, stood up and toddled over to get a closer look! Our mums couldn't believe it. It's definitely true though – they've got the photos to prove it. They've got a whole stack of the most embarrassing shots on their phones that they just love to show people.

So yeah, Hannah and me finish each other's sentences and she knows me better than anyone. She's not afraid to tell me when I'm wrong about something AND she can tell when I'm getting a crazy idea in my head. She just rolls her eyes and says, 'here we go again', but I know she's with me. Oh, here she is now:

HB: Hey J. How r u?

JM: Fine, just chillin.

HB: Me 2. Can u make CC?

JM: Can't wait!

CC stands for Coding Club. It happens after school and we've learnt loads of cool stuff already. The only bad thing is that Lindy Lawson goes. I don't even think she likes coding, she only comes to annoy me. Last week she got her screen to flash Jenny Many is a dweeb over and over until Miss Pearson saw her and made her say sorry. I could tell you lots more about Lindy Lawson. But I won't.

Where was I? Oh yeah, my friends! So ... as well as Hannah, there's Ella. I'm really lucky that she lives right next door. If I want to hang out with her, I just go up to my treehouse and flash my torch – on off, on off, on off – and she can see it from her bedroom. If she can come over, she flashes back the same signal. If she wants to come round but her dad says she has to do homework, she flashes back on off, on (swirly circle) off, on off.

Ella has this thing with animals. They just love her! I think it is because she's really calm and gentle. She loves them, too. She can seem shy sometimes, but that's only when she's around grown-ups or daydreaming. When she's your friend she's really funny and chatty. She's also a green belt at karate, so don't ever let her catch you being unkind to a kitten or bullying a bunny!

The last person you need to know about is Dylan. Dylan Wilkins. He's one of my favourite people because he's just so ... WEIRD! He has these crazy words for stuff. When it's your birthday, he won't say 'Happy Birthday' like everyone else, he'll shout 'Felicitations' instead.

Here's what Dylan sent me after my soccer game last week:

JM: Did you see the game?

DW: Yeah. Great goal, Jenny!

JM: Thanks. Top corner always works!

DW: A real humdinger!

Humdinger! He cracks me up. Dylan doesn't play soccer, which is probably a good thing because he's one of the clumsiest people on the planet. But he's such a great friend he never misses my games. He also knows everything there is to know about superheroes, which is always handy if you want to find out, say, where to find Kryptonite.

So that's my friends. You'll meet all of them in this story and I guess you'll get to know a lot more about me too, because I'm going to tell you about something really

AMAZING that happened to us this summer. It's what you'd call an adventure. There are clues and codes and runaway pets. Trust me – it's a rollercoaster of a tale.

Oh, hi Trixie. This is Trix. She's my dog. You'll hear about her, too. She's super-cute, and really smart. Right now she's tugging on my shoelace – it's what she does when she wants to tell me something ... oh yeah. The soccer.

• • •

2

Planet Thrill

It all started when I was on my way to soccer.

It was a Saturday afternoon and Mum and me were walking over to the park. The team I play for, Pennyvale FC, had a match against the Moon Bay Dolphins. Trixie was with us, trotting along on the lead, sniffing bushes and wagging her tail.

'Can I see your phone?' I asked

Mum. 'There's something I want to show you.'

I don't have my own phone yet, but my parents are pretty cool at letting me borrow their phones or tablets to message my friends or look stuff up for school projects. I also take LOTS of photos and videos of Trixie.

'Look Mum,' I said, tilting the screen so she could see. 'How cool is this?'

Trixie's face was staring out of the video, her nose close-up.

'Trixie!' my voice came from the phone. 'Blink once for yes, twice for no. Ready? OK, so ... are you a good girl?'

Trixie blinked once.

Mum giggled.

'Trixie? Do you like baths?'

Two blinks.

'That is hilarious,' grinned Mum.

'Last question, Trixie,' came my voice again. 'Would you like a doggy treat?'

The biggest doggy blink EVER told me that was a 'yes'! On the screen my hand tossed a gravy bone into Trixie's mouth, then ruffled her fur.

Mum gave me a hug. 'So funny, honey,' she said. 'That's an upload for sure.'

Mum loves Trixie as much as I do. I mean, who wouldn't? She's adorable. That's why she set up an account on Instagram all about our superstar dog. It's called @Fluffadoodle. We post photos, drawings and funny clips of Trixie all the time. There are a lot of pet lovers out there too, @Fluffadoodle has 371 followers already.

When we got to the park, Coach Carlos hurried us into his team talk. We were going to have to play hard in this match – the Dolphins are a tough side. When he'd finished, we put in our hands and did our 'PENNYVALE Power!' shout.

The game was fast from the start. Their goalkeeper was massive and we missed from two corners. Mia Sanchez passed to me and I started running up the pitch at top speed, looking for an opening on the wing. Zoey McBride was right there. She's really fast, but sometimes she gets a bit over-enthusiastic. I passed to her and WHAM! She walloped the ball so hard it soared way past the goal and out of the gates of the park.

And that's when I saw it ... just

outside the gates, a man on a ladder was plastering a gigantic poster on a billboard. The picture showed the biggest rollercoaster, a giant water flume and a laser ride. There were words, too:

Coming Soon
PLANET THRILL
Live your dreams!

I must have stood there for ten minutes gawping at that poster. The ball was in my hands, but I forgot about the game. A new theme park was opening in town and it looked A-MA-ZING.

I mean, I've been to fairs before. Pennyvale has one every year, but all it has are hook-the-duck stalls and an ancient bouncy castle. No splashy log flumes and definitely no mega-roller coasters. I knew right then that I HAD to go.

After that, the rest of the game was a bit of a blur. We won two-one, but I didn't score and I missed some easy chances. I just couldn't stop thinking about how it would feel to zip around bends, plummet downwards at a million miles an hour and loop-the-loop on the rides at Planet Thrill.

Back home the smell of melting chocolate hit me the minute I opened the door. Dad was baking up a storm in the kitchen. My dad loves to cook. Dylan calls him Captain Cake and swears he's the best superhero ever – a suit-wearing businessman by day, an apron clad avenger by night.

'Dad!' I shouted, dumping my kitbag in the hall. 'Please can I borrow your laptop?'

'Well hello to you too, Jenny,' Dad replied, wiping his chocolatey hands on a tea towel.

'Sorry,' I giggled, giving him a hug. 'Hi Dad. Would you mind if we log on to your computer? There's a new theme park opening and I need to know all about it right now because we absolutely have to get tickets and they might get sold out if we don't hurry ...'

'Whoa there,' Dad chuckled. 'I can hardly keep up! This sounds pretty urgent. Give me a second and we'll take a look.'

Dad peered at his cake through the oven window then got out the laptop. We found the site straight away. Clicking through the slideshow of images was even more jaw-dropping than seeing the poster. There were rides where you stood up, rides where gravity pinned you to your seat while the floor dropped away, and others that whooshed you up into the clouds.

'See?' I whispered. 'It's so cool! We just have to get a pass and then we can go like, all the time.'

'That would be cool,' said Dad. 'Now let's see ...'

He clicked onto the visitor page. Beneath the kitchen counter I crossed my fingers on both hands. I held my breath and waited.

'How much?' spluttered Dad.

'How much is it?' I asked.

'TOO much, Jenny,' said Dad, shutting the lid of the laptop and putting an arm around me. 'It's a small fortune. I could refit the kitchen for the cost of a family annual pass. I'm sorry, hon.'

'But Dad,' I pleaded. 'It would be good value. I'd go all the time.'

'You'd have to be there all day every day, sweetie,' he shrugged. 'In fact, you'd have to live there.'

'I would, Dad, honestly. I'd go with my friends and we could hang out there every weekend. You won't regret it.'

'Sorry Jenny, it's just too expensive. Maybe we could look at a trip later in the year for your birthday.'

Dad shook his head then went back to his baking. The discussion was finished.

So that was that. My life was over. I was never going to get to

Planet Thrill, even if it was down the road.

They might as well have built it on Mars.

• • •

Flumes and Flakes

It turned out I wasn't the only
person buzzing about Planet Thrill
– at school the next day you
couldn't hear anything else. As
soon as I walked through the gates
the chat was 'flume this', and 'laser
that' and, 'so when we are we
gonna go?'

'Jenny!' called Hannah. She was
sitting under the apple tree on the
far side of the playground. As

usual, there was a book propped up on her lap.

'Hey.'

I dumped my backpack and slumped down beside her.

'What's up with you, Grumps?'

One annoying thing about Hannah is that she is *always* in a good mood. Literally NOTHING gets her down. Even when she got stung by a bee on the school trip and her eye swelled shut, somehow she still managed a smile. 'It's not the bee's fault,' she had said, 'stinging is a natural instinct.'

This thing Hannah has – I don't know what you'd call it, her 'up-ness' or something – is great most of the time. But when something has gone really wrong and everything is basically ruined ...

'*What's up?*' I repeated back to

her. 'Oh, nothing much, just the worst thing that has ever happened to me in my whole life. Ever!'

Hannah arched one eyebrow. The corner of her mouth curled up a tiny bit. 'Really?' she said.

'Really,' I sulked.

'What? Worse than the time you tripped over my foot in the canteen and face-planted into your spaghetti Bolognese ... in front of the whole school?'

I couldn't help but chuckle at that. Two years on, the shame had finally faded enough for me to be able to recall the memory without wanting to be physically sick, although even now, I could still feel my cheeks going a bit hot. I have to admit that it was pretty funny though. I had pasta strings hanging off my eyebrows!

'OK, so not that bad,' I giggled, 'but still pretty grim. There's a new theme park opening.'

'Planet Thrill?'

'You saw? Yeah. Planet Thrill!' I grabbed hold of Hannah's shoulders. 'Doesn't it look AMAZING?'

'Awesome!' nodded Hannah.

'Incredible!' I continued. 'But Dad says passes are too expensive and that I might be able to get a ticket to go for the day ...'

I tailed off. Lindy Lawson and her two sidekicks, Emily and Jane, glided past. Lindy looked over, narrowed her eyes then turned and whispered something sneaky to Emily. Suddenly all three of them burst out laughing.

Hannah, apparently hadn't noticed.

'I don't understand?' she said.

'What are you moaning about? You still get to go.'

'... ON MY BIRTHDAY OR CHRISTMAS!' It was just too much. 'That's at least six whole months away, Hannah. I can't wait that long. I'll be practically an adult!'

'Well,' said Hannah, 'you'll be ten years and eleven months old to be precise. I think they'll still let you in.'

I sighed. This was not the point and she knew it. I've never been what you'd call 'patient'. 'Live your dreams' the poster said. I couldn't wait six months to do that!

'It's just ages away,' I muttered.

'Actually,' said Hannah, shouldering her bag as the bell rang, 'it's only one hundred and eighty-two and a half days away.'

Did I mention that Hannah is

scarily good maths?

'Not helping,' I said. I got up and followed her towards the classroom.

'So that's only twenty-six weeks,' Hannah continued to herself. 'Or four thousand, three hundred and something hours.'

See what I mean? Maths genius.

Mrs Norris was halfway through the register when Dylan finally ran in. He looked like a hamster who had decided to take a run on its wheel mid-meal.

'I'm 'orry, 'issus 'orris,' he spluttered, spitting crumbs out of stuffed cheeks as he scrabbled for his desk.

'See me at break, Dylan,' said Mrs Norris. 'Jessica Wheeler, are you here or not?'

'What the what?' I asked as Dylan stuffed himself into the seat beside me.

'Star flakes!' he whispered. 'Got to eat them all the time now. As much as I can cram in.'

With that, a flurry of crunchy cereal shapes splattered onto my open science book. I gave him a weird look.

'Sorry,' he gasped, back to non-hamster size. 'That new park thing, Planet Thrill, has a deal on. They're doing tokens on the side of Star Flakes boxes. If I can collect twenty-five coupons, I'll get half-price entry!'

'Brilliant!' I said, brushing my science book clean and thinking that, with Dylan's liking for snacking, he might even manage fifty. 'This is amazing news. You could save up. I hate Star Flakes, but I'll give you my pocket money for extra packs if you'll take me, too.'

'Course,' whispered Dylan as Mrs Norris shot him a warning look.

We both reached for our pens.

'We've got a deal, D,' I grinned. 'Get chomping.'

• • •

Dog-Robatics

Dylan, Hannah and I spent the rest of the day imagining which ride we'd go on first and which one would probably make Ella (who doesn't even like riding bikes too fast) throw up. Ella's in the other class, but we couldn't see her at lunchtime to check our theories because she was busy doing eco-monitoring. We didn't get together until the end of the day at Coding Club.

'Hi everyone,' said Miss Pearson as we took our places, two to each screen. 'We're going to spend this session thinking up some great ideas for this term's animation project. Get into your groups and I'll come around and see how you're getting on. I'm just popping to the staffroom to see Mrs Norris first. Back in a tick.'

Dylan, Hannah, Ella and I moved our chairs together.

'Anyone got any ideas?' said Hannah.

'Unicorns,' replied Ella.

'Astronauts,' I suggested.

'Superheroes!' Dylan piped up.

Hannah wrote the ideas down.

'Maybe we could make a cartoon where the hero flies over a rooftop or something?' Dylan added.

'I think ...' Ella began. But we

never got to hear what Ella thought because suddenly she was cancelled out by Lindy's screeching tones.

'So yes,' she squawked, 'I'm definitely getting an annual pass to Planet Thrill. Daddy says he knows someone. He might even be able to get us VIP passes so we get on the rides quicker. Queuing is so lame!'

On our side of the monitors Dylan stuck his tongue out and pretended to barf. I tried not to snort too loudly.

'That's so cool, Lindy,' simpered Emily.

'What if I'm the first person to ever go on that mega water ride?' she said, loud enough for everyone to hear. 'They might rename it the Lindy Log Flume!'

That made Lindy's little fan

club crease up. I rolled my eyes. Ella mouthed, 'blah, blah, blah.'

'I'm just super-lucky like that I guess. My parents give me pretty much anything I want. Look what I got at the weekend.'

A hand was thrust high into the air, accompanied by loads of cringy "oohs" and "aahs". A golden locket dangled from the fingers. Lindy wanted to make sure that everyone knew exactly how much her darling parents adored her.

'Gorgeous isn't it,' she bragged. 'It was REALLY expensive. But I guess if you want nice stuff you have to have the money to pay for it ...'

That was enough. 'Can't you just be quiet?' I said, standing up and glaring at the group of girls over the tops of the computers.

'Some of us are trying to work here.'

'Yes,' muttered Hannah. 'Let's get on with our animation.'

'Oh dear, jealous much?' sneered Lindy. 'I guess Jenny doesn't-have Many treats.'

All three of them squealed at that. At the next screen, James Devine and Mo Salim started sniggering too. This got me hopping mad.

'I'm not JEALOUS!' I cried. 'Why would be I jealous of you and some stupid, fake ...'

But I didn't have time to finish my sentence. I was going to tell her that I didn't care about her gold locket (although I wouldn't have been able to say the same about the VIP Planet Thrill pass), but right then, Miss Pearson came back into the ICT suite.

'Jenny Many!' she said. 'I'm surprised at you! If you can't work properly and be respectful of others you won't be welcome at Coding Club anymore.'

My face turned a hideous shade of scarlet. I sat down, seething.

'We should definitely do the superhero animation,' said Ella, pushing her glasses up her nose. 'We can show the hero zapping a villain called Lindy Lawson.'

But no one mentioned the animation for a few days. Dylan was too busy stuffing Star Flakes. He'd started putting handfuls into his packed lunch and coat pockets, so his mouth was too full to talk most of the time. Ella was off with a cold. Hannah and I spent most of our time talking about the sleepover we were planning. Even though it was fun, I still felt mad about being blamed for causing trouble in Coding Club.

When I get like this, the only thing that calms me down is spending time with Trixie. I decided to take her to the park and throw some sticks. She always jumps much higher than you think she's going to – sometimes she looks as if she is weightless for an instant, floating in the air.

I found a nice chewy stick, then hurled it as far as I could. Trixie loved it. She hared back with it in her teeth again and again. Then, all of a sudden, she leapt so hard she flipped over and landed back on her feet. I laughed and had another go, throwing the stick so that she had to reach behind her head as she leapt. It worked again.

'That's amazing,' came a voice behind us.

I looked up. Dylan was heading over with his friend, Harvey.

'I wonder if Bonza can do that?' said Harvey. Bonza is Harvey's beagle. He's almost as cute as Trixie. Almost. Harvey chucked the stick and Bonza bounded into the air. He didn't flip, but his ears flapped sideways, making him look like a furry helicopter.

Something sparked in my brain.

'Dylan!' I bellowed. 'This is *it*. Our animation! We could do dog-robatics! Funny clips of dogs jumping around. It could be totally, utterly brilliant! We could add sound and a surprise ending. We could even make a dog-robatics website with a puppy name generator. This is **SO COOL**. See ya!'

I was off. I sprinted out of the park back towards my house, tugging Trixie along behind me. I couldn't wait to get started! This was going to be the best animation ever, even if I did say so myself.

As he watched me disappear into the distance, Dylan sighed and pulled out the phone his mum always gave him when we went out on his own. He punched in Hannah's number:

DW: Uh-oh.

HB: Uh-oh what?

DW: Just seen Jenny. She's had an idea.

HB: What this time?

DW: Our animation. It's the next craze.

HB: Another one of her itises. Help!

DW: Gadzooks!

HB: ????

DW: Never mind.

Of course *I* didn't know at the time they were discussing my tendency to get mega-obsessed with my own brilliant ideas – I was too busy at home in my room. I had to draw, write and plan everything to make our animation a dazzling, dog-robatic reality!

• • •

Team Trixie

The next weekend was the
sleepover. Usually I'm jigging from
leg to leg at the front door,
listening out for the sound of Mrs
Banerjee's car as it swings up the
drive, but this time around Mum got
there first.

'Come in!' I heard her say, 'Cup
of tea? Slice of lemon drizzle?'

Mum ushered Mrs Banerjee
through to the kitchen. 'Go on,

upstairs, sweetie,' she told Hannah. 'Jenny's been up there for hours, I'm not sure what she's up to but it seems to involve a *lot* of stationery. She's been raiding the desk in my office all morning.'

I heard footsteps on the stairs and then Hannah appeared. Her eyes were squeezed tight shut.

'I hardly dare look,' she said in a dramatic voice. 'What are you up to, Miss Many?'

Slowly, she opened her eyes.

'Jenny!' she gasped. Her knees seemed to give way a little, making her cling onto the doorframe. Hannah blinked and looked around her, trying to take everything in.

My entire bedroom had been transformed into an animation studio. I had decorated it floor to ceiling with ideas for our Coding

Club project. There were sketches
of Trixie plastered all over my
pinboard and scribbled-on
storyboards scattered across the
desk, spilling onto the rug. The
mirror and door to my bathroom
were almost completely covered
with stickie notes. There were
bullet-pointed lists, colour-themed
mood boards and magazine cuttings
featuring different dog breeds. I
had been VERY busy.

'Well,' breathed Hannah after
what seemed like several hours.
'This most definitely qualifies as an
"itis."'

Hannah always says that when I
get an idea in my head, it spreads
like there's no stopping it. It's
quicker than catching a cold. That's
why she calls them my "itises".
There was the time I tried to stop

the local council from selling our town park – *greenitis*. And the time I decided to become a world champion skateboarder – <u>*boarditis*</u>. The list goes on and on.

'I got it,' giggled Hannah. 'Animatitis!'

'I know it looks bad,' I said, 'but there's some genius stuff here.'

I told Hannah all about my brilliant dog-robatics idea. She looked pretty impressed by the time I'd finished. When I showed her the clips of Trixie and Bonza doing their tricks, she was sold.

'We're going to make the best animation ever,' decided Hannah. 'Lindy Lawson will definitely lose it when she sees how cool this is!'

I laughed, but I didn't want to waste our Saturday night thinking about Lindy. We did some more brainstorming, then we headed out into the garden with Trixie. We all climbed onto the trampoline and filmed her barky bouncing on Mum's tablet. Later, Dad fired up the barbeque and made us homemade burgers and slaw. We were both tucked up in front of the telly with pjs and popcorn when the advert came on.

Laser beams at
PLANET THRILL
Laughs and screams at
PLANET THRILL
Live your dreams at
PLANET THRILL!

Photos of happy kids and families flashed across the TV

screen. Music blasted with a cool, catchy beat.

'Look!'

Both me and Hannah yelled and sat forward at exactly the same time.

The ad cut to a smiley presenter. 'The Planet Thrill website is launching today,' she announced. 'Check in and join our interactive, intergalactic treasure quest!'

We listened, mouths open, as the presenter described exactly how the quest would work. Entrants would need to register then follow clues to discover secret locations. Along the way they had to log their progress, submitting pics and videos of every stage online.

'The fastest seekers to complete the trail will win annual

VIP passes to Planet Thrill. That's free entry with VIP perks for one entire YEAR. Happy hunting, Thrill Seekers!'

The ad finished with an awesome action shot of the park, packed with beaming visitors, whooshing rollercoasters and laser lights flashing in neon colours. I was so psyched I dropped my bowl of popcorn. It went everywhere. We raced to pick it all up before Trixie could tuck in. Human food is not good for dogs.

'We have to register, now!' I breathed, scooping handfuls back into the popcorn bowl.

'Right now!' agreed Hannah.

We ran to find Mum and told her everything. When we'd both calmed down, she agreed that we could log on and enter.

'We'll create a group profile, girls,' said Mum, 'but you're not to use your photo.'

She typed the URL into the search engine for the Planet Thrill website. Mum and Dad are really strict about staying safe online – that's why on our @Fluffadoodle account you never actually see my face.

'Trixie can be our mascot!' I cried. 'Use her picture instead.'

'Yeah, Team Trixie!' cheered Hannah.

Mum found a cute doggy photo and I uploaded it, typing in Team Trixie as our entrant's ID. A box flashed up on the screen:

Team Trixie is officially registered as a Thrill Seeker

in the Planet Thrill Treasure Hunt.

Hannah and I hugged.

'Let's tell the others,' I said. 'Is that OK, Mum?'

Two minutes later we were on a group video chat. Ella and Dylan's faces appeared in the top corners of the screen. Dylan's cheeks were massive – I could hardly hear him speak over the noisy crunch of Star Flakes. I had to admire his dedication. He had decided that eating his bodyweight in cereal was a solid plan B if we didn't win the Planet Thrill tickets.

Ella kept popping in and out of the camera, jumping up and down on her bed like a loony.

'I love treasure hunts!' she squealed. 'Mum always does a trail for my Easter eggs, but this is SO MUCH better. When do we start?'

'As soon as we can,' I said.

'Mum says hundreds of people are going to enter so we shouldn't get our hopes up. I don't think she gets how much we like rollercoasters!'

'Yeah,' agreed Hannah. 'We *have* to win these tickets.'

'Team Trixie are on a mission!' shouted Dylan. 'Bring it on!'

• • •

Broccoli-Gate

On Monday morning at first break
Team Trixie met up under the tree
in the playground. We quickly
added a new member, Harvey,
because Dylan wanted him to join.
We like Harvey and we figured that
five brains would be better than
four. He was in.

'When do you think the first
clue will come out?' asked Ella.

'Soon,' I announced. I *hoped*

rather than knew this, but the opening was only six weeks away and it made sense that they would want to give people enough time to find the secret locations.

'I wonder what kind of clues there will be?' Harvey said. 'Pictures? Riddles?'

'Maybe numbers,' said Hannah, her eyes shining. 'Maths puzzles would be the best.'

There was a loud rustle behind us.

'Be alert!' hissed Dylan. 'An eavesdropper lurks beyond.'

'Hmm?' I said. I love Dylan's funny words, but sometimes I haven't a clue what he's on about.

'Our fellowship draws the gaze of an undesirable,' he said more fiercely, signalling towards the tree.

'And in *English* please?'

Emily Greene stepped out from behind the trunk munching on a bag of crisps. She smiled knowingly, then ran off towards Lindy and Jane.

'NOOOOOOO!' we all shouted at the same time.

We knew exactly what would happen next, and sure enough at lunchtime it did.

We were in the canteen wondering why it was broccoli pasta bake *again*, when Lindy pushed her way past us.

'That's right,' she said over her shoulder to Emily and Jane. 'We're down as Lindy's Lovelies. I've already phoned Dad and got him to register us, so we're in.' She flashed her expensive mobile phone around – which isn't allowed in school anyway. 'I used that picture of me from last summer where my hair is really long. Don't worry girls, I think you two are there in the background somewhere. We're bound to win. Mum and Dad will just drive us wherever we need to go in the Jag. It's really fast.'

This was too much.

'You'll have to decode the clue first,' I blurted out.

Two hundred faces turned to gawp at me.

'Did anyone hear something?' sniffed Lindy, looking as if a bad smell (other than the whiffy broccoli bake) was wafting under her nose.

'I didn't,' squealed Jane. Emily shook her head frantically.

'I said, "you'll have to work out the clue first."'

I scrabbled to my feet, pretending not to notice that the canteen had suddenly gone quiet. 'It's not just a case of driving fast. You need to have the brains to know where you're driving to!'

'Sit down, Jealous Jenny!' sneered Lindy. 'Who asked for your opinion?'

'No one,' I said. 'But why are you even entering at all? I thought you said dearest Daddy had got you VIP tickets already. Or was that a LIE?'

Lindy huffed and swished her hair, then quickly turned away. I sat down.

'That told her,' laughed Harvey, slapping me on the back.

Normal levels of chatter rose up again and everyone returned to their green pasta. We finished up and went outside.

'Fancy kicking the ball about for a bit?' said Harvey.

'Sure,' I answered.

But five minutes' later, when I was just about to take a shot at goal, Ella ran up.

'Jenny! Jenny!' she said breathlessly. 'Listen! Lindy has really got it in for you. I was clearing my tray away and I heard them talking. Lindy says that she doesn't care about the treasure quest tickets really. All she wants to do is make sure you don't stand a chance of getting the prize.'

'The sneaky little ...' I broke off, stunned.

'Foul play!' yelled Dylan from the bench. 'Down with them all!'

It seemed like decoding clues would not be the only battle we had to face. Team Trixie was also going to have to deal with another obstacle – a small, dark-haired, super ANNOYING one. Lindy Lawson.

That night I climbed up to my treehouse. I needed some time to think and get over Broccoli-Gate. It's cool up there in the evenings, and quiet. The rustling leaves and birds have a knack of calming me down when I've got a head full of Lindy Lawson. I was just lying back on my beanbag imagining me and my friends running through the gates of Planet Thrill when Mum's voice called down the garden.

'Jenny! Jenny, honey. Come inside. You're going to want to see this.'

I poked my head out. Mum was

standing by the patio doors with a big grin on her face.

'The new Planet Thrill ad is on telly,' she said. 'The first clue is out!'

• • •

7

Moon Mission

I was so desperate to see the TV I didn't even wait to sit down. Instead I threw myself in through the patio doors and dived headfirst over the back of the sofa.

'Feet off the cushions!' Mum chuckled as I scrabbled to get myself upright again.

There was a burst of light then a huge splash of water filled the screen. The foam cleared and the words Lunar Flume flashed up. I gulped. It was only the biggest, longest, steepest, scariest water ride I had ever seen! The living room filled with the delighted screams of all the lucky riders. The carriages climbed up and up, held still for a moment, then plunged back down through a magical lunar landscape at hold-on-for-your-life, gasp-for-air speed. There were soaring dunes, dazzling star systems and deep moon craters. At the very end, the carriages splashed into a huge lunar lake, soaking everyone on board. It was completely, totally and absolutely awesome!

The ad cut to a close-up of the same presenter who had announced the treasure quest. This time she was dressed in a shiny space suit.

She put her visor up to talk.

'Hello, Thrill Seekers!' she waved. 'Lucie Lewis coming to you live from the Lunar Flume ride at Planet Thrill. So here's where things get serious. Are you ready for your first clue?'

'I'm ready! I'm sooo ready!' I yelled. My entire body was buzzing with excitement.

A beat came on and Lucie began to say a rhyme. As she spoke her words popped up along the top of the screen:

First you must download the PT app,
You'll find coordinates and a map.
If you need a boost there's something more:
Seek a lunar sea and a sandy shore.

71

'Here!' Mum thrust her smart phone into my hand. 'Snap a photo so you can remember the whole clue.'

I grabbed the phone and clicked. 'Can we get the app, Mum?' I asked, watching Lucie Lewis take a seat on the coaster and glide off over a moon dune.

'Of course,' Mum replied. 'I've already checked. It's free to download.'

I did a search and found the Planet Thrill app straightaway. Within moments it was showing up on Mum's home screen.

'Here it is,' I gasped, 'Oh! The map is huge. It must cover a hundred miles. And what are these? They just look like a load of numbers.'

'Those are the co-ordinates

that will help you pinpoint an exact location on the map,' Mum explained. 'Why don't you work on Lucie's clue first, I think that should help.'

"Kay, right.' I said, flicking back to the photo of the rhyme. '"Seek a lunar sea and a sandy shore." Hmm ... *lunar sea* ...' I tailed off.

'Not ringing any bells?' said Mum.

'No! And in any case it's a bit of a misleading clue because there are no seas on the moon,' I said, pouting. We had done this in science. 'There isn't any surface water at all up there – it just evaporates under the sun.'

'I think you have to suspend reality when it comes to theme parks, honey,' smiled Mum, squeezing my shoulders. 'And anyway, you're getting off track. You need a *real* place, somewhere on the map where treasure could be hidden.'

'Somewhere where there are lunar seas and sandy shores. Well,' I said, thinking it through, 'seas and sand – that sounds like the beach! It must be on the coast somewhere!'

'Could be ...'

'But Lucie said *lunar* seas.'

'That's right,' said Mum, egging me on. 'Think about it.'

'Lunar means "moon". So we're talking about moon seas?' I stopped for a minute. 'I've got it!' I yelled, grabbing Mum around the neck so hard she made a little cough. 'It's Moon Bay! Lunar is like the moon and a bay is full of the sea, isn't it?'

'Uh-huh!' Mum nodded.

'And Moon Bay has a beach!' I checked the map. 'Moon Bay is marked right here. Do you think the coordinates could take us to the exact spot?'

'I think you've cracked it, honey!' Mum smiled. 'Right, I've got to get the oven on.'

'This is amazing, Mum,' I said. 'Can we go now? Straightaway?'

Mum shook her head. 'Jenny, we're not going to get stuck in rush-hour traffic jams all the way down to Moon Bay just so you can hunt around in the sand in the dark.'

I felt like I'd just blown an amazing triple bubble from one of those wands and that Mum had seen it, admired it and then popped it.

'But Mum!' I howled. 'Do you know how many people will have seen that clue? We have got to start IMMEDIATELY.'

Mum eyed me over the book she'd just picked up. She had her 'firm face' on. No good ever comes when she does that look.

'I said "no".'

Never mind popping my bubbles, now I felt like Mum had poured the whole bubble mixture down the sink. I folded my arms, but really I knew that sulking wouldn't get me anywhere. 'Can I at least ring Dad?' I begged at last, 'just to tell him that I've cracked the clue?'

Mum nodded. 'If he doesn't pick up, you're not to keep ringing though,' she warned. 'You'll have to wait until he gets home.'

I dialled Dad's number and waited. He answered straight away. I could tell that I was on the car speakerphone.

'Hi Jen! All OK?'

'Hi Dad. Guess what?' I didn't wait for him to guess. 'The first Planet Thrill clue just came on the TV and I've already cracked it!'

'Great stuff!'

'Yeah, it's Moon Bay,' I continued. 'The first treasure item is hidden right now in Moon Bay!'

'How exciting! Oh, hold on, hi Arthur!' I heard the horn beep twice. 'Sorry Jenny, that was someone from work. I'm really chuffed for you.'

'Can we go then? When can we go?'

'To Moon Bay?'

'Yes to Moon Bay' I was

exasperated now, but I tried not to show it. ' Can you take us Daddy? Pleeeease!'

I never call him Daddy unless it's an *extreme* emergency – and he knows that. I let the words hang hopefully in the air.

'Hmmm ...' Dad was at least thinking about it. 'There is a new cake shop in Moon Bay. I've been meaning to check it out for ages. I have a little window in my schedule on Sunday afternoon. Would that work for you?'

'Yes!' I punched the air. 'Thank you so much. I love you, Dad.' I glanced at Mum and she mouthed "guacamole" back at me. 'Oh, and it's fajitas for supper. Mum says can you get some guacamole from the shop? Byeee!'

I hugged Mum again then asked

if I could bike round to Hannah's house. I couldn't wait to tell her everything. Team Trixie's moon mission had officially begun!

• • •

Dune Walk

The next few days lasted f-o-r-e-v-e-r. Finally, eventually, after the longest Saturday IN HISTORY, we made it to Sunday lunchtime. The sun was shining and you could just tell it was going to be the best day ever. We picked Hannah up first, and then Dylan. Harvey was spending the day at his grandma's. Ella had to stay home so she could help out at Robbie's birthday party.

Robbie's her brother. He's really sweet and he's still only little so it was kind of an important day. So there were just five of us in the car – six if you count Trixie, and I do always count Trixie.

Mum drove and Dad was put in charge of the car stereo. He played some of our favourite tunes, turning the volume up so loud it made us giggle. We all started to groan when he decided to put some of his golden oldies on next, but after a while even we couldn't resist singing along. The best one was Elvis Presley crooning *Ain't Nothing But A Hound Dog*. Trixie loves Elvis and that is her FAVOURITE track – for obvious reasons. She started howling away to the music, like she always does when she hears it. It's super funny!

I made sure to film a clip, but it's definitely tough on the ears.

After an hour or so of car karaoke we turned into a zigzaggy road that picked its way down the side of a grassy cliff. A sweet little seaside town was waiting at the bottom. The sun glinted off the waves and caught the windows of the brightly painted houses. I rolled the window down and took a deep breath of the salty air. It smelt like seaweed and mystery. Just perfect.

We parked up and Dad went off to hunt for his cake shop.

'Hang on a minute,' said Mum said, struggling to get Trixie's lead on. She handed the lead to Hannah, then took her phone out from her pocket. 'You'll need this,' she said. 'You kids go on, I'll be walking right behind you.'

'This is so cool!' Hannah laughed, as we crowded around her, waiting for the map and coordinates to pop up on the screen.

'I think it's this way,' I said, pointing in the direction of a path leading down to the ocean.

'I concur,' said Dylan.

I raised one eyebrow at D – it's one of my talents.

'That means I *agree*,' he explained.

We pointed Mum's phone at the path and set off. It led us right through Moon Bay's famous sand dunes. Clusters of zingy-bright flowers pushed their faces into the sea breeze, tucked in amongst bobbing grasses. A lizard scuttled past. We slid and rolled along the wind-blown ridges at the top down to the troughs at the bottom. It was more sheltered here and the air was still, muffling the sound of the waves.

After a while of hiking through the sand, we decided to take off our hoodies and tie them around our waists. I glanced at the screen. The coordinates had disappeared, but a flashing red point had appeared on the map just a few metres from where we stood. We were getting closer.

'This way!' Hannah said. She tumbled down a dune towards a little gate leading onto the beach.

Trixie might not be able to see a map or use a phone, but she DEFINITELY has a nose for treasure. She began barking and tugging at the lead. She launched herself down the dune as if she were a speedboat and Hannah, now travelling on her knees, was a water-skier being dragged in her wake.

'It's here somewhere!' I said, scrabbling down behind them. 'You OK, Han?'

'Y-eugh-p,' spluttered Hannah, spitting sand out of her mouth.

Dylan, Hannah and I gazed after Trixie. The pup already had her nose to the ground, snuffling intently and wagging her tail.

'Look!' yelled Hannah.

Trix started to dig furiously at a clump of bushes nestled around a fence post.

We ran over and there it was. Just waiting for us! My heart was thumping so fast I thought it was going to burst out of my chest.

A tiny safe had been fixed to

the side of the fence. It was tucked right at the bottom, half-covered in sand. There was no mistaking the logo though. Planet Thrill was emblazoned in gold letters on the door. There was also a funny bar code printed underneath it.

'How do we open the safe?' asked Dylan.

'With this,' I told him. The phone now showed our location to be exactly over the dot and, as if by magic, a symbol of a treasure chest popped up on the screen. I held the phone out in front of the door, as if I was helping Mum to scan a barcode on a packet of crisps at the supermarket. There was a funny little "beep" and it popped open.

'Wow!' we all gasped at the same time.

'Wow!' said Mum, finally catching up with us. 'Those dunes are steep.' She stopped for a moment and took in the scene. 'Oh my. You've done it, guys!'

I opened the door wider. Inside was a little box filled with miniature toys and gifts.

'We have to take one, I think,' said Hannah.

I chose a tiny porcelain moon. It was a purple fridge magnet – a souvenir of our find. While I turned it over and over in my hand, Dylan counted up the rest of the toys.

'Lots of other people must have been here already,' he sighed.

I nodded. The box was only half full.

'It doesn't matter,' said Hannah, looking hopefully up at Mum.

Mum's eye twinkled. 'You still

got here,' she reminded us. 'That was a pretty successful day's work, I'd say!'

Mum has a habit of being right about stuff. It had been an awesome adventure and we were ready for clue two. We spent the rest of the afternoon having fun on the beach. Trixie went for a swim, but it looked a bit rough and cold for us so we buried Dylan in the sand instead. Then we headed up to the esplanade for some ice creams. We were walking along enjoying our double choc-chips with sprinkles when I spotted two tall girls and a smaller one jostling to get their places in a group selfie.

    'No, not you. This one's just of us two.' The darker of the two taller girls gave the smallest a shove so that she disappeared out of the shot. The girl stumbled back, then swung round to face us.

Lindy!

I looked away quickly so Lindy wouldn't see me staring, but couldn't help sneaking one more glance back. The two big ones had to be the sisters she was always gloating about – Cara and Josie. They were still preening and posing in front of their phones, obviously taking gazillions of pics. Lindy looked sad and a bit lost. As we turned off the boardwalk I heard her speak:

'Can we go on the big wheel in a minute, Cara?'

'Oh stop whining on, Lindy,' her sister snapped. 'Fairs are for babies.'

'I can't believe Mum said we had

to bring her,' grumbled Josie.

We headed back to meet Dad. For a moment, I felt sorry for Lindy. Then I thought about all the mean stuff she did to me every day and the feeling faded away.

We tipped sand out of our shoes and climbed into the car. And then it came to me.

'I've just had an off-the-charts amazing idea,' I suddenly told Hannah and D.

Hannah narrowed her eyes. 'Even if you do say so yourself.'

I pretended not to hear that. 'We should put our Coding Club animation skills to work,' continued. 'We could film a little Trixie cartoon with each upload to the Planet Thrill site. It will really make our entries stand out.'

'You could use your *Hound Dog*

singing clip,' smiled Mum.

'That is quite brilliant,' Hannah had to agree.

'We've got to do it, Jenny! gasped Dylan. 'Splendicious plan! Oh, and Mrs Many? Please can we stop and pick up another box of Star Flakes on the way home?'

That boy!

• • •

Rocket Launch

Back home I just couldn't wait to get started on the upload to Planet Thrill. My idea of adding a funny Trixie cartoon had been inspired by watching Lindy's sisters' little photoshoot on the boardwalk. It felt weird seeing people being horrible to Lindy for a change. She hadn't looked like normal Lindy. Something was different about her. She seemed smaller and sort of ... less *shiny*.

Anyway, I didn't want to waste
time thinking about that. As I was
scrolling through the clips of Trixie
at Moon Bay a message beeped. It
was Ella.

ED: Wanna come round
and eat cake?

JM: Duh! What do you think?

ED: Well? Can you come or not?

JM: What flavour cake is it?

ED: Snake sponge with fox frosting!
(only kidding, it's rainbow cake)

JM: My fave. Be there in 5.

I asked Mum to send the best
Trixie clips to Ella's parents' email
address and then ran out the door.
Two minutes later I was back again.

'Mum! Did we get anything for
Robbie? It's his birthday?'

Mum handed me a round, gift-
wrapped parcel. It was definitely a
football. She's great with birthdays,
Mum. She never forgets anyone,
even if it's a second cousin's
aunty's brother-in-law, there'll be
something from us ready for their
big day.

Ten minutes later, Ella and I
were in her kitchen, stuffing pieces
of rainbow cake while Robbie tried
his best to smash ornaments with
his new pressie.

'Hey, Ronaldo! Shall we take that outside?' said Mr Davis, making a spectacular save in front of their tropical fish tank. He gave us a wink and grabbed Robbie's sticky hand.

Ella's mum had set the laptop up on the kitchen island. Ella logged on, found the email from my mum's account and dragged the video clips onto the desktop. She opened them up, one by one.

We watched Trixie singing to Elvis, Trixie dragging Hannah down the sand dunes and loads of the pup leaping happily in the sea.

'I'm so gutted I missed out,' said Ella.

'Me too.' I pulled a sad face. 'It was great, but we missed you.'

'So you think we should try to animate one of these clips when we upload on the Planet Thrill site?'

'Yes! I mean, we're called 'Team Trixie'. It makes sense to have our mascot involved in the quest, doesn't it?'

Ella nodded. 'Which clip should we try to do?'

I frowned. 'Mum suggested the ones of Trixie singing, but she liked them so much she's used one on the Fluffadoodle account already, so I think ...' I leant over, grabbed the mouse and opened the movie showing Trixie digging for treasure like a mad thing. When the dog sat back up, her nose was completely covered in sand and she couldn't stop sneezing.

Ella snorted with giggles. 'Brilliant!'

Ella's mum let us call Dylan, Hannah and Harvey so we had a quick video meeting about the plans. Everyone agreed it was the perfect way to get people interested. Ella and I spent the next couple of hours making our own mini animation, trying to remember all of the things Miss Pearson had shown us in Coding Club. I messaged the others every time we got stuck. Ella did a great drawing of Trixie, then we used code to make her paws move just like she was digging. Harvey and D helped us add music, then Hannah wrote a funny caption that popped up at the end. Honestly, if you could see it when we were done – Team Trixie's movie was SO COOL it seriously deserved a red carpet premiere!

As soon as we were finished, I raced back home and asked Mum to help me upload the clip to the

Planet Thrill site, along with pictures of our safe souvenir. Stage one of the competition was officially complete!

As I lay in bed that night listening to Trixie snuffling away in her basket I couldn't even THINK about sleep. Instead I imagined myself exploring Planet Thrill, climbing onto the Lunar Flume, laughing with my friends and eating fries in the Space Café. A picture of Lindy Lawson trailing behind her sisters floated into my head, but I pushed it away again. I wanted to think happy thoughts. The adventure was just beginning. I couldn't wait for clue number two.

It turned out that I didn't have to hang on too much longer. The following Wednesday Dad called me down to breakfast earlier than normal.

'What's up, Pa?' I grumped, rubbing the sleepy dust out of my eyes. 'Do I have to walk to school today? Are you not taking me?'

'I am taking you, but you're going to want to hear this.' He pointed at the radio. Dad always listens to the radio in the morning. There's a show he likes about food called *Grow Your Own*. I reckon it should be called *Groan And Moan* instead. It's just people phoning in to complain that slugs have eaten their lettuces and they drone on for hours about how their green beans have gone stringy. Luckily, we were on an ad break. A bubbly voice came out of the speaker:

'Lucie Lewis here. Live from the Rocket ... *aaaargh!* ... from the

Rocket Launcher. It's the latest spectacular ride at Planet Thrill. I'm halfway to space already, but here's your next clue!'

Lucie got her breath back, then started to rhyme:

At Planet Thrill there's tons to do,
So check the app to find clue two.
The map will show the place to go,
A visit helps to makes brains grow.

'Happy questing, Thrill Seekers!' said Lucie, bringing the ad to a close. 'We can't wait to see your uploaded clips on the Planet Thrill website.'

The radio crackled and a much deeper voice began talking about turnips. I turned to Dad, repeating the end of the rhyme over and over so I wouldn't forget it.

'A visit helps to make brains grow. What do you think that means?'

'What sort of place can you go to make your brain get bigger and stronger?' said Dad, scooping up a spoonful of porridge.

'You could visit somewhere like a restaurant or a zoo, I suppose.'

'You could,' repeated Dad unhelpfully.

I sat down and thought hard. 'But where can you visit to make your brain grow? I guess that means somewhere you learn stuff?'

Dad nodded.

'Like a school or the university?'

'Maybe,' Dad shrugged.

'But why would you visit a

school you didn't go to?' I muttered to myself. 'Where else can you learn stuff? Oh!' It came to me in a flash. 'A museum!' I was practically shouting now. 'You learn stuff in a museum ... but which one?'

'There are a few in the city,' agreed Dad. 'What ride was she on again?'

'The Rocket-*aaaargh*-Launcher!' I said with a cheeky grin, doing an impression of Lucie Lewis trying to read her lines whilst being launched into space at the speed of light.

'And where could you learn about things like space?'

'The Science Museum!' I shrieked. 'It's so obvious!'

'You got there in the end,' Dad chuckled.

'Can we go on Sunday again?'

Mum clip-clopped into the

kitchen dressed in her suit and heels – she had a meeting today. She looked as if the slightest thing (like tipping orange juice over her shoes while trying to film Trixie – it was an accident, HONEST) could set her into a spin.

'Sunday's out, Jen,' she said, flipping through papers in her briefcase. 'Lily's coming over.'

Lily is my cousin. My 'older' cousin, as she likes to tell me literally every time she visits. She's Auntie Jackie's daughter. And that, basically, is the best thing about her. I'm kidding – not. OK, I'm *slightly* kidding. Lily is all right really. It's just that she's a cello playing sports superstar who can also do advanced algebra. She's only eleven!

Normally I quite like it when

Lily comes, once I've listened to all her amazing achievements and we can just, well, *hang*. But not THIS weekend. Not on Sunday. No way!

Mum and Dad said this was what they call a 'non-negotiable' fact and that they would take me to the museum the weekend after. I didn't think I could BEAR IT. How many thousand people would have made it to the second safe by then?

• • •

Curse of the Cousin

I didn't want to be in a gloom, but it is hard to smile when you can see your future as a prizewinning Thrill Seeker disappearing down a big BLACK HOLE. Sunday came round soon enough, but that just made things worse. I tried to cheer up, I really did, but it was torture to be stuck at home when everyone else was out, roaming the city, hunting down the second clue. Dad tried his best to take my mind off things. He even gave me one of the red velvet cupcakes he'd whipped up especially for our visitors – my absolute all-time fave of his bakes – but it was hopeless. Team Trixie was in a bad place.

Uncle Gary's car pulled into our drive just before midday. Lily jumped out dressed, as usual, as if she was headed for the Paris catwalk. Lily, to use my Mum's words, 'does not do casual'. Even if she knows full well that we're going off-road biking on the forest trail round the back of our house she will turn up wearing sequinned shoes with heels and a full-length lace ballgown. It's not that she doesn't look great. She does, if you're into frills and faux-fur and fashiony stuff. But sometimes Lily is just a bit … *much*.

'Hey girlfriend!' she beamed, giving me a hug and a kiss on the cheek, re-applying a coat of sticky pink lip gloss straight afterwards.

'S'up cuz?' I replied, unable to return her hug as she was already tip-tapping upstairs towards my bedroom. I waited at the foot of the stairs. I knew what was coming:

'What the … ? Jenny! Quickly,' shrieked Lily. "Something TERRIBLE has happened. I think your room's been burgled!'

I sighed and went upstairs.

'See!' Her mouth hung wide open, making her look just like an extremely hungry trout.

'No, this is all me, Lily, ' I giggled. 'It's an animation project I'm working on for Coding Club. These are all my ideas for how it's going to look.'

Lily tiptoed in, hopping from the doorway to the rug as if the place was full of litter. She began nosing around, flipping up paper, dislodging sticky notes and checking out my drawings.

'Actually these are pretty good,' she said, picking up some of my Trixie sketches. But then, in the blink of an eye, Lily's interest faded again. She moved on to one of her favourite subjects instead.

Nails.

'Do you like the colour?' she asked, holding out a carefully manicured hand. 'It's called "City Slicker".' Lily inspected the silver nails for the trillionth time that morning, then flashed me a satisfied smile.

'Guess so,' I mumbled. I wanted to be nice, but the only thing city-related I wanted to hear about was the Science Museum. Where I was supposed to be. Right now. With my BEST FRIENDS. Searching for the second clue.

'What's up with you today?' Lily frowned.

That made me feel bad. I mean, Lily and me don't have that much in common, but she *is* family. I decided to tell her.

'I'm sorry,' I sighed. 'I'm just a bit distracted. I'm trying to do this treasure quest thing. It's an amazing competition to win tickets to a theme park and the second clue's out there and Mum and Dad won't take me to the location until next weekend by which time it will probably be miles too late to get anything out of the safe.' It came out in a big wave of words, like when you turn on one of those electric showers full blast, but then it takes a minute for the water to pump up to the head and start gushing. WHOOSH!

Lily nodded. 'Planet Thrill? Yeah. I saw that's opening. Think Mum's ordered us a family season ticket. Chris'll probably want to go. I'm not bothered.'

She actually sounded *bored*. It was so unfair. Literally everyone in the world was going to get to go to Planet Thrill before me! Lindy Lawson. My cousin Chris. Who next? Was five-year-old Robbie next door already on the VIP list? Were there some field mice living in the woods at the end of the road that were right now filling in their family passes – 'small mammal discount' included?

'Do you think I could go in your place?' I asked Lily hopefully.

'I don't think so. We had to give loads of information – photos and everything.'

'Well we are cousins, there is a bit of a family resemblance.'

'Er ... I don't think they'd believe you were me,' said Lily huffily. 'I'm nine months older than you and your hair's frizzy.'

Rude.

The rest of the afternoon went OK. We hung out in the treehouse and then Mum took us to the Smoothie Shack, although it took ages to get there because Lily had to look in the window of like, every shop.

After she'd gone, I took Trixie out on a long walk. I usually love walking because it's brilliant brain time where I get loads of cool thoughts and ideas, but this time the only picture in my mind was of loads of hands rummaging through the Planet Thrill safe at the city museum.

Still, one cool thing did happen. When I got a treat out for Trixie she stood up to beg for it and I accidentally tripped backwards over a tree root. I didn't fall, I just staggered back, and guess what? Trixie walked towards me on her back legs! Not a couple of steps, but eight or maybe even nine! I rewarded her with the treat and then tried again.

Go Trixie. She repeated the trick all over again. My pup can walk! How awesome is that?

At school the next day I hardly even managed to get my coat off before Lindy started. She was practically BELLOWING to the entire year that she and her sisters had solved the second clue *and* already uploaded their find on the Planet Thrill site.

'It was soooo easy,' she boasted. 'I mean, a toddler could have cracked it.'

I got busy rummaging around inside my backpack, pretending to search for my pencil case. My head was shoved right inside it, trying to drown Lindy out.

It didn't work.

'Did you hear that, Jenny Many?' said Lindy, tapping me on the shoulder. '*I said* I've found clue two. Have you?'

I knew she knew that we

hadn't. I had seen her talking to Dylan as we came in through the gates. Dylan's neck was blotchy and red. D does not like it when girls that are not me or Hannah or Ella insist on talking to him – because of the red neck thing and because he can't get his words out the way he likes to.

'All under control, Lindy Lawson,' I said, trying to sound breezy and un-bothered. 'Team Trixie solved the clue ages ago. We're just waiting for the rush to die down and then we'll just rock up and log our entry.'

'I wouldn't wait too long, if I were you,' Lindy smirked. 'The safe was already half empty. It is a competition you know.'

Jane Sparkes helpfully chose that moment to pipe up as well.

'Yeah, better hurry up,' she snorted. 'There aren't MANY treasures left to find!'

My name. The gift that keeps on giving. Thanks Dad.

The thing was, Lindy and her lurkers were actually right. By the time we arrived at the Science Museum the following Saturday, headed for the space floor and found our way to the exact hiding spot, TONS of other people had beaten us there. We knew they had because there were so many clips on the website – including Lindy's video. She stood holding a shiny coin up the camera, until she got elbowed to the side by Cara and Josie, pouting and flicking their hair like a couple of overgrown poodles.

When Ella finally opened the

door to the safe there were only two teeny trinkets left – a postcard of a planet and a tiny metal flying saucer. We took the flying saucer and hurried home to upload it, along with a brill animation of Trixie walking on her hind legs as if she was chasing after it.

We took so long to get the sequence right Mum invited Ella to stay over. She came up with late night milk and cookies for our midnight feast (which, as a family tradition always happens at 9pm before teeth cleaning – a bit lame, but kinda nice anyway). We showed her our upload.

'I'm impressed, girls!' she said. 'OK I put this on @Fluffadoodle as well?'

We both nodded.

'Light's out by ten,' she smiled,

turning down the light. 'Thrill-seeking-treasure-hunters need their sleep.'

• • •

The Weasel Has Landed

The following Saturday I was in my room practising my clarinet, trying to check my finger placements on the Internet, when a message suddenly popped up on the screen.

Video Call Request:
Dylan Wilkins

I clicked the green icon. Dylan's face popped up.

'Mmm ... greetings and salutations!' he said, beaming from ear to ear.

'Hi!' I said. 'Are you chewing on something?'

Dylan held up a cereal packet. 'Those Star Flakes are not going to eat themselves Jenny,' he reminded me.

'Right ... Anyway I can't really chat. I've only got Mum's tablet in my room because I'm practising my Grade Three pieces.'

'Weasel time again, is it?'

I stuck my tongue out. D insists on calling my clarinet 'the weasel' because when I first started playing I wasn't very good. It's pretty tricky, the clarinet, because there's this thing called a reed and you have to get it in the right position when you blow or else you'll make a dreadful screeching sound. The first time I played my clarinet to Dylan he said it sounded like a weasel in its death throes squealing 'weeeeasel, weeeeasel, weeeeasel!'

Even Dylan's insults are funny. He was right, too – I really wasn't good back then, but I am getting better.

'Have you heard anything about the last clue?' Dylan asked.

I turned stiff with fear. 'No! Did we miss it? This is AWFUL! We've missed it and now I'll never get to Planet ...'

'Jenny!' Dylan blurted out. 'You haven't missed anything. I haven't seen or heard anything and neither has anyone else that I've spoken to. Harvey and Hannah are watching four TV channels each to check for ads and Ella's got the radio covered.'

'Thank goodness for that,' I breathed. 'For one minute I thought you were going to tell me that it's all over and Lindy Lawson won the competition.'

'It isn't over until the horizontally gifted lady sings.'

I sniggered – I wasn't sure exactly what Dylan was on about but he sounded hopeful that we were still in the running, so that was good enough for me. We chatted for another few minutes. Dylan was planning to visit Harvey later. Harvey's dad had promised to take them both fishing. We signed off so D could put on his wellies and get going.

'Jenny!' Mum suddenly shouted

up from the living room. 'The Planet Thrill ad is on!'

I flew down the stairs three at time, my clarinet still tucked under my arm.

This time Lucie, the presenter, was nowhere to be seen. There were no sweeping shots of Planet Thrill or dramatic close-ups of the rides. Instead a strange voiceover that sounded like an alien from outer space told us that the park would be opening in one month's time and that tickets were available through the website. I edged closer, hanging on every word.

'The Thrill Seekers' treasure quest has triggered a mega-galactic, record-breaking online response,' continued the alien. 'Well done, humans! Stay alert and near to your TV. The last clue will be released very soon.'

The screen filled with a collage of photos. More and more popped into view, a mosaic of uploads from the hundreds of wannabe Thrill Seekers all across the land.

'Pause it!' I screamed at Mum, making a lunge for the remote control.

'Please ...' she warned. Mum plucked the remote out of my hand, then gave it a gentle click so that the image froze on screen.

I began scouring every millimetre, looking for a sign of Team Trixie. There, in the bottom left hand corner was Lindy Lawson, mostly hidden by her sisters, but there nevertheless. I also recognised a group of girls from my soccer team and a boy called

Thomas Moxley who used to go to our school. But Team Trixie. We were ... *nowhere*.

'You can turn it off,' I muttered. 'It's not the final clue anyway.'

I felt rotten. The fact that our pictures hadn't even made the cut seemed like a seriously bad sign. There had been so many faces there. So many people, just like me and Hannah, Ella, Harvey and Dylan, all wanting to experience Planet Thrill. I decided to head back upstairs and carry on weaselling.

'Jenny! look!'

Now it was Mum screaming. She had pressed play.

I turned to see the pictures swipe away. Instead of lots of tiny faces, a funny Labradoodle puppy was walking on its hind legs across the screen. My heart started to thud really fast, but it took a nanosecond for my brain to catch up. Our Team Trixie logo flashed up in the corner and then I blinked and it was gone again.

'Aliens and ETs, spacemen and now *space dogs*! All of these Thrill Seekers can't wait to get to Planet Thrill,' said the alien voiceover. 'How about you?'

I put down my clarinet. For a second there was absolute silence. Then three things happened all at once. Mum's phone beeped with a video call request. The home phone started to ring and – *ding-dong!* – the front doorbell went. Every single member of Team Trixie was calling at the same time!

'Did you see it?!' I cried, putting Hannah's call on speakerphone as I hauled Ella in through the front door and hugged her tight.

'We're famous!' Hannah screamed, nodding her head furiously.

'Hi Dylan, yes oh and Harvey, too. Wait a sec, I'll put you on,' said Mum, opening up her laptop. 'It's all gone a bit crazy here.'

She wasn't wrong. Team Trixie must have spent at least twenty minutes whooping and screaming at each other. It was brilliant!

That afternoon everyone came over – even Harvey and D put their fishing trip on hold. We hung out in the treehouse for hours, talking and laughing. Hannah had a new trick where she curled herself really tight into a kind of a ball, so Harvey invented a new game called

'Rollerkid'. It was just as silly as it sounded. We used our coats to mark out a pitch then took turns to roll Hannah up and down the lawn, collapsing into fits of giggles as we tried to get her into the goals.

'I don't want to interrupt a great match,' coughed Dad politely, looking up from his garden chair, 'but I think you should take turns at being the ball.'

'Yes,' said Mum. 'Hannah is going to get sick if she keeps rolling around on the grass like that.'

Hannah popped up. 'I'm fine, honest,' she said. 'We've tried using Dylan but his arms and legs are too long to tuck in properly. Harvey's too tall to push. Jenny's already had a turn and Ella says her mum will go mad if she goes home with grass stains all over her new leggings.'

We had pizza for tea. Luckily the delivery guys were happy to do lots of toppings on one fifteen-incher because we all like our pizzas just-so. Me and Harvey stick to margherita. Ella likes ham and pineapple. Hannah pours hot chilli sauce over every slice and Dylan only eats pizzas sprinkled with anchovies.

Anchovies. That gets me every time. Fish. On a pizza. *Really?*

We must have been on our third slice each when the clue finally came up on the telly. We had been sat in a row along the kitchen counter eating and watching a cool show about penguins when the ad break came on. Ella did a funny squeal and tugged on my arm, pointing up to the TV on the wall.

'Lucie's back!' she urged. 'It's gotta be time!'

I nearly spat out my orangeade. Lucie Lewis was standing, microphone in hand, beside a glittering Ferris wheel with dozens of golden cars hanging all around the frame. The wheel was turning round and round in a slow circle whilst colour laser beams flashed and arced across the sky behind it. It was the most GIGANTIC ride I had ever seen – miles bigger than anything else in the park.

Lucie cleared her throat.

So Thrill Seekers,' she said. 'The time is nigh, the time is now. If you want to secure your VIP pass and access all of the epic rides in Planet Thrill, including the Golden Orbiter here, you've got to complete the last stage of your mission. Can you crack the clue and find the final location? The first to complete the quest and submit an upload to the Planet Thrill website will be the winner. Could it be you? Why not?'

Me and Harvey shared a nervous glance.

The camera zoomed in on Lucie's face. Now her voice hushed to barely a whisper:

'It's all to play for BUT you'll need to pace it right. The safe will only be placed at the location at one specific time. Paying attention? OK, let the countdown begin ... '

Team Trixie all leaned forward together, our eyes pinned up at the screen.

'Ten, nine, eight ...' said a booming voice. Clips of the Golden

Orbiter, the Rocket Launcher and the Lunar Flume flashed across the screen. 'Seven, six, five ...' I gripped Hannah and Ella's hands and held on tight. 'Four, three, two, one ...' A spacecraft blasted off, filling the screen with smoke. When the cloud cleared, neon pink letters were revealed, glowing in the night sky.

So now the end's in sight,
it's time to think,
Set off to reach your goal
then watch it sink.
Its stunning daily show
should bring good cheer,
The source of life for all
who dwell right here.

There was only just time for

Mum to take a snap of the words before Lucie reappeared one last time, waving happily.

'Happy hunting, Thrill Seekers!' she beamed. 'See you soon at Planet Thrill.'

Pizza time was over. We scrambled out to the treehouse so fast, the five of us nearly tumbled on top of each other.

'Help,' groaned Harvey. 'I'm stuck on this clue already!'

'Where do you think it could be?' wondered Ella.

We studied the coordinates on Mum's phone. The points seemed to centre on a green area inland, away from the town and the coast. There didn't seem to be any buildings around.

'Don't panic,' I said. 'Let's work

on the clue. *The end's in sight.*
Well that's easy. It means we're
nearly finished with the treasure
quest.'

'Or does it?' replied Hannah. 'It
could mean that we need to look
near the end of something.'

'What has an end?' asked Dylan.
He started chewing thoughtfully on
his nails. 'A path maybe, or a road?'

We were stumped. Every time
we tried to find an answer, we
came to face to face with another
question.

'What about the *watch it sink*
bit?' I continued. 'Why would our
goal sink?'

'Maybe the safe's in a boat?'
suggested Hannah. 'A boat could
sink.'

We all nodded.

'A daily show could be

something to do with a theatre, couldn't it?' chipped in Dylan.

'Or a circus?' added Ella.

'And the *source of life for people who dwell here*,' I said. 'That seems like it could be air.'

I checked the phone again. My head was starting to seriously throb now. 'The coordinates are pointing inland. So... what we need is a place inland, maybe a theatre or a circus, where there's lots of air and a sinking boat.'

There was a very, very, very, long silence. You could practically hear our brain neurons fizzing. Fizzing then puttering out into ... *nothing*.

We kept going round and round in circles. We tried our best, but it was beginning to get dark and we still had nothing to show for it.

Dylan was the first to give up. 'I think this is just too tricky for us,' he sighed. 'We are not all born to be victorious.'

'Don't say that!' I shouted. 'We've got as much chance as anyone else. We are not quitting!'

Dylan frowned. He hates raised voices. I think it's because of how it was at his house before the divorce. 'I've got to get home,' he said quietly, sliding off of his beanbag.

'Ella!' A voice called over the next-door fence. 'Home now, please.'

Harvey checked his watch. 'I better get off, too,' he frowned.

We all climbed down the treehouse ladder feeling as flat as a stack of Dad's banana pancakes.

'Bye,' I huffed as Dylan, Harvey and Ella headed out of the gate.

'Don't worry, Jen,' said Hannah, as we watched them go. She gave my arm a squeeze. 'I'm sure we'll crack it.'

I shrugged and forced a smile. I knew Hannah meant well, but right now Team Trixie couldn't crack so much as an egg, let alone the winning clue in a treasure quest.

• • •

In My Dreams

I was running along a long path with Hannah, Ella and Harvey. Dylan wasn't anywhere to be seen, but for some reason I didn't feel worried. We were going full pelt. Sprinting with the wind blowing us along. And even though the road was steep and Ella's legs are much shorter than mine (she says running is her worst thing – apart from egg sandwiches) she was keeping up easily. We ran all the way to the top of a hill, then looked down to see a beautiful lake below. We watched a flock of birds take off from the water's edge. I blinked in surprise. The creatures seemed to be incredible, bright green flamingos. The birds soared into the sky, lit up against an enormous, golden sun.

One of the birds landed near us. Somehow it folded its legs and squatted down. I looked at the others and gasped. The bird was laying an EGG! Hannah tiptoed towards it and carefully caught the egg in both hands. Then things got seriously weird:

The bird turned towards us and it had Dylan's face! Suddenly Hannah cracked the egg over my head. The yoke slid down my face and Dylan squawked 'Winners!'

I woke up with a start. A shaft of golden sunlight streamed through the crack in my curtains. Trixie was lying next to me on the pillow. She had drooled on my head.

'Eeew!' I grabbed a tissue from my bedside cabinet and tried to rescue my soggy hair, still thinking about the dream. Despite the fact that Dylan had been a flamingo and Hannah had attacked me with his egg, it had been a good one. I'd felt relaxed. I'd been with friends and it had been a really beautiful place. The sun, the lake, the birds ... the SUN!

I sat bolt upright.

'That's it!' I cried out to Trixie. She had jumped off the bed and was now standing by it, paws resting on my covers, with an eager expression on her little face.

'The sun is a golden orb!' I knew I was right. I had to be. 'It's the source of life for everyone on Earth. Without the sun's heat and light nothing could survive here. And ... oh, this is massive ... ' I leapt out of bed and started pulling on clothes. ' ... it *sinks* every day when it sets.'

I was only half-dressed, but that was a minor detail. I leapt down the stairs two at a time. Mum and Dad were already in the kitchen. Dad was reading the paper while Mum made ... eggs.

'Morning, honey,' said Mum. 'You're up with the lark this morning.'

'I'm up with the flamingos!'

'Really? No eggs-in-bed today?' asked Mum.

I always have breakfast in bed

on a Sunday. It's my weekly treat. 'No time for lie-ins!' I cried. 'I know where the last clue is. Do you remember that nature place we went to last summer? When we had the twilight picnic by the lake?'

'The Wetlands Reserve?'

'Ah yes,' nodded Dad, putting down his paper. 'We watched the sunset together! That was a lovely day. We should do that again.'

I nodded. 'I am DEFINITELY going to do that again, Dad. Today!'

Mum and Dad were looking right at me now. The corner of Dad's newspaper curled into his coffee and then an odd, burny smell started coming off the stove.

'The last clue!' I explained, urging them to keep up. 'It's about the sun. And the Golden Orbiter at Planet Thrill, remember? The clue talked about it being a source of life.

'Clever girl,' Mum said, giving me a hug. She sprang back and snatched the pan of over-scrambled eggs off the hob. 'Oh! These are for the bin!'

I didn't mind. I wasn't that hungry anyway.

'You know the line, *reach your goal and watch it sink*? We thought it was talking about a boat, but it can't be, can it? It must be the sun sinking every night. The *stunning daily show* is the sunset. I can't believe it took me this long to work it out!' I was so happy, I couldn't help laughing at the same time.

'You did it!' smiled Dad, giving me a high-five. 'I knew you would.'

'In my dreams,' I said.

'No, you really worked it out!'

I shook my head. 'I mean that I worked it out in my dreams, Dad.' I told my folks everything that had happened in my head. They cracked up laughing when I described flamingo-Dylan laying the egg!

After breakfast Trixie and I went straight over to Hannah's house to share the news. Her eyes nearly popped out when she heard about my dream.

'So I cracked it right on your head?' she asked. 'Mean!'

'Nah, I think it was because your words about cracking the clue were the last thing I heard before I went to bed last night. They kind of stuck with me. And you were right, weren't you? I have CRACKED it.'

'You definitely have,' Hannah

agreed. 'Let's go and do some research on the computer.'

We headed into her parents' office and booted up the PC. It was pretty old and slow, but we got there in the end. Hannah looked up the website and started to read:

'"The Wetlands Reserve is one of the most important nature conservation areas in the country,"' Hannah began. '"Its stunning main lake is a wonderful haven for all kinds of wildlife. A visit at sunset is particularly spectacular."'

'*Stunning daily show*,' I breathed. 'That's where the safe is. I bet you a zillion quid it will only open if we go at sunset.'

'No bets needed,' said Hannah. 'We can't just turn up whenever we feel like it. Lucie said that the safe would only be there to find at one special time. This has got to be when the sun is reflected in the water. Like a golden orb!'

'Yessss, Hannah!' I punched the air. 'We've got to fetch Ella, Harvey and Dylan!'

'Ella and Harvey will be up for it,' Hannah said quietly. 'I'm not sure about Dylan.'

I raised an eyebrow. I suppose I had been pretty snappy with him last night.

'Do you mean he might not come because he's annoyed at me?'

'Nope,' she grinned, standing on one leg and flapping her arms. 'I mean that he might be NESTING!'

That afternoon we hung out at Hannah's house, planning every element of the quest. After a TON of texting and group video chats, all of our mums and dads finally agreed between them that we were allowed to go to the reserve to watch the sunset. The decision was that we could take our bikes as long as we stayed to the cycle route.

'Do you think many other people will have cracked the code?' asked Ella.

'Indubitably,' replied Dylan. We looked at him blankly, until he added, 'Definitely, yes.'

'Even if they don't work out the actual sunset part, they will be able to get nearby using the coordinates,' I said. 'We've got to make sure we stand out in the crowd – in case anyone from Planet Thrill is filming.'

'Any ideas?' Hannah asked.

'I could always paint our faces,'

suggested Ella. 'I can do us all as Trixie-dogs.'

My heart started doing that thing again when it pounds at three hundred miles an hour. 'Ella Davis,' I whooped. 'That is totally BRILLIANT!'

Ella is a face painting EXPERT. Anything you want – butterflies, superheroes, cool, scary stuff for Halloween – she can do it. The Planet Thrill people already had their eye on Team Trixie. This was a genius way to show them our star qualities, without giving away our true identities.

Ella rushed off to find her paints. Within half a minute I was sitting down with my hair scraped back having my base colour applied. By five o'clock we were all set. Hannah grabbed a camera.

'Mum!' she shouted. 'Can you take a picture of us?'

Five pups and Trixie posed for a shot – there was no stopping us now!

We biked as fast as we could. The closer we got to the Wetlands Reserve, the more the cycle route filled up with people. Families and children wobbled along the trail, chattering excitedly about 'clues' and 'treasure' and the 'lake'.

By the time we got there, the sun already looked heavy and low in the sky. It washed everything in a warm, golden glow. It was just like in my dream – except Dylan wasn't covered in green feathers.

'We made it!' grinned Harvey, doing a quick Trixie impression. 'Ra-uff!'

We pushed our bikes together then did a quick face paint inspection. Dylan's whiskers had started to run down his face after he got puffed out on the ride and Hannah had clearly had the sneezes because her black doggy nose was all smudged, but we still looked kind of cool.

'To the lake, post-haste!' said D, leading the way.

We wheeled our bikes to the bike store, then jogged over to the shore of the lake. Groups of people were sitting and picnicking all around the water. Some were pointing binoculars at clumps of reeds, others were paddling about in the shallows, but no one seemed that interested in the sunset.

'What do we do now?' wondered Ella.

But I didn't have to answer. At that very second, the sun sunk down to touch the place where the land meets the sky, far away in the distance. Its reflection shimmered on the lake like a giant, golden penny. Everybody in the Wetlands Reserve oohed and aahed together, mesmerised by the sight.

Hannah was the first to speak.

'We need to go,' she urged. '*Now*.'

'Good point,' said Harvey. 'This is the time to find that safe. Have you got the map and coordinates up, Jen?'

'Yes,' I nodded, pulling out my mum's phone. I checked the screen. A red dot had already started winking on the map. 'Over there,' I said, pointing to the other side of the lake. 'Come on!'

I began to move away, until Dylan pulled at my sleeve. 'Jenny. Where's Trixie?'

Where was Trixie? She'd been right THERE, snuffling around in the reeds. We called her and we called her, but she didn't come.

The bestest dog I ever had, our lucky mascot, was gone.

. . .

Lost and Found

'Trixie!'

'Here, puppy!

'Trixie, Trixie, TRIXIE!'

We searched the whole way around the bank of the lake. We called her name, we held out treats, we asked everyone we passed if they had seen a little labradoodle, but no one seemed to know anything. It was like my pup had vanished into thin air. I tried to be brave, but there was a churny feeling in my tummy and a lump in my throat that I couldn't swallow away. Where was Trixie?

'I have to find her,' I told the others. 'We need proper help. I'm going to go and ask at the reception.'

'Good idea,' said Ella. 'I'll come with you.'

'No, I'll be fine, it's right there. You lot head in the direction of the safe. We've all worked so hard to get to this point. We're so close! Come on Ells, swap phones.' I took Ella's phone and handed her mine, showing her the little winking dot on the map. 'Call me if you spot Trixie on the way. If you don't, take a treasure from the safe and then meet me at reception.'

'At least let's find a staff

member first,' said Hannah, taking charge. 'Your mum and dad wouldn't want you wandering off all alone.'

Harvey ran up to a uniformed reserve ranger and asked her to take me to the main desk. As soon as they knew I was OK, he joined the others running in the opposite direction. 'We'll be right back,' he shouted over his shoulder. 'I promise!'

'Having a good day?' the ranger asked as we walked towards the wooden buildings at the entrance to the park.

'We were until Trixie went missing,' I replied, desperately trying not to cry.

'Don't worry, I'm sure she'll turn up,' smiled the ranger. 'We have staff all over the reserve, they'll spot a stray dog in no time. Was she off-lead?'

'No!' I said. 'I've seen the signs. She has a collar with a tag engraved with our phone number. And she was on her lead, I just dropped it.'

'The excitement of the treasure quest?' nodded the ranger.

'The sunset, actually,' I said. 'It was mega.'

The ranger smiled and pushed open the door to reception. The staff inside listened carefully as I told them all about Trixie. I showed them a photo from Ella's phone.

'Cute!' said a lady with a cap and hoop earrings. 'Trixie, huh? Reminds me of that cartoon dog they had on TV the other day. Anyone see the Planet Thrill ad?'

'That's HER!' I spluttered.

The lady patted my shoulder. 'No, this wasn't a real dog, sweetie,' she said, 'It was just a cartoon, but it did look a lot like her.'

'No, that really is our Trixie, we ...'

But before I could explain that I was part of Team Trixie and that it was us that had made the dog animation, the phone in my hand buzzed. Ella's voice was breathless. 'She's here. Found ... TRIXIE.'

The phone line was cutting in and out, but that didn't matter. Now I really did burst into tears.

'Oh! That's amazing,' I blubbed, smiling and nodding at the rangers to let them know it was good news. 'Where was she?'

Hannah came on then. 'She was safe,' she giggled, 'at the safe!

Clever dog sniffed it out. She was waiting right next to the box, wagging her tail. She wanted to show us that she'd found the treasure!'

'Told you, she's one in a million!' I laughed. 'Did you get a treasure from inside?'

'Yes, a little clay bird. There was loads of stuff in there ... I think we must have been one of the ... it's really hidden away ... we ...' The line was going again.

'That is the best news,' I gasped. 'We need to get home ASAP so we can upload the find onto the Planet Thrill site.'

The nice ranger who had led me to the office tapped my shoulder, 'Remember that the tickets go to the first finders!' she said. 'If you don't want to wait until you get home you should upload it from here.'

'Yes,' agreed cap lady. 'The phone signal's terrible around most of the reserve except at the top of Heron Hill. If you have 4G you should be able to upload from there.'

I rushed towards the door. 'Thank you so much,' I blurted out. 'For everything!'

I made my way back around the near side of the lake. We were nearly there. Team Trixie – every member of Team Trixie – had worked together to make this happen. Before I knew it, there was Harvey giving me a massive wave. Dylan hurried along behind him, doing a big thumbs up sign. Ella was next, holding Trixie tightly on the lead, and then Hannah, grinning back at me and clutching something precious to her chest.

We were only metres away from each other when I heard it – a soft snuffling sound coming from the bushes a little to my left. I peeked over the tops of the leaves. There was a little wooden bench set beneath a willow tree, circled by trailing branches above and grasses all around. It was the perfect spot to sit without being seen, to listen to the rustling leaves and have a good think.

Unfortunately the person sat there right now wasn't doing that. Instead they were having a good cry.

I stood up. A girl was hunched up on the bench, knees up to her chin, sobbing softly into her jeans.

The sight made me instantly take a step back. It seemed wrong to disturb her. I didn't want anyone to think I was spying.

But as I tried to tiptoe away again without making a noise, the stranger sniffed loudly and reached into her jacket for a tissue. She looked up at just the wrong time.

'You!'

I was face-to-face with Lindy Lawson.

• • •

Friends Forever

Before I could do or say anything at all the rest of Team Trixie turned up and started leaping all over me.

'Hey Jenny!' hooted Dylan. 'Hunting for flamingos in the bushes are we?'

I stepped away quickly, trying to fake a laugh. 'No, nutter! I just thought I saw Trixie's dog tag.' It was feeble, but it was all I could come up with.

'Trixie's tag is still on her collar, Jenny,' said Ella. 'Look.'

'Oh yeah,' I replied, leaning down and studying it in an attempt to seem like I'd really believed it had got lost.

'Ta-dah!' cried Hannah, opening her fingers to reveal the trinket from the safe. 'Time for the finder's photo!' She fumbled inside my backpack for the extendable selfie stick.

'OK,' I said, 'but let's turn towards the lake. The light's better.'

Everyone turned away from Lindy's hiding place, giggling and shouting as they tried to organise themselves for the picture. I am sure I heard the faintest sigh of relief come from the other side of the bushes. I scooped Trixie in my arms and hugged her tight. Hannah held the clay bird up in one hand and the selfie stick in the other.

'Say *Trixie!*'

We all grinned like Cheshire cats.

'We'll need to upload this right away,' Hannah announced, like any of us needed reminding, 'to give us the best chance.'

'Right,' I nodded. 'The ranger said we need to go up Heron Hill. It's the only place to get good phone reception around here. It's that way, see?' I pointed up towards the highest point in the reserve.

'Come on, then!' shouted D, already striding away.

I tried not to look too shifty. 'I'll just be a minute. I need to go to the loo first.'

'I'll wait with you,' said Ella.

She's super-kind, Ella but you do have to work hard to shake her off when you need to be alone. I wasted at least five precious minutes trying to persuade her to follow the others.

As soon as Ella and the others were out of sight I ducked inside the branches of the weeping willow. It was lovely in there, sheltered but still warm from the sun.

'Don't worry,' I whispered to the crouching figure. 'No one saw you.'

Lindy sniffed.

'Are you OK? Well, you're obviously *not* OK, but ... '

There was a long pause.

'I'm not telling you,' Lindy whispered at last. 'You'll just blab to everyone.'

I stood up to go. 'Fine,' I said, taking one last look at her blotchy frown. 'I was only trying to help.'

Lindy burst into tears again. I stopped. Waited a bit. Then I had to ask.

'Is it about the competition?'

'There are more important things in life than a treasure hunt,' Lindy sobbed angrily, covering her eyes with her hands.

We sat there without speaking for a while, waiting for Lindy's sobs to ease off. I wondered how it was possible to feel sorry for someone who had been your sworn enemy since forever. But Lindy didn't look like Lindy right then, she looked small and sad, just like she had on the boardwalk. It was a bit like handling a stray kitten, I thought –

a tiny, vulnerable ball of fur that could also give you a stinging scratch for no reason at all.

'I've lost my necklace!'

The words came out like a strangled scream.

It took me a minute to catch up. 'What? The really expensive one your dad bought you? The one you had in Coding Club?'

Lindy nodded miserably.

'Can't you just get another one?' I suggested. 'You said your parents buy you anything you want. Maybe they won't mind?'

Tears streamed down Lindy's face. Then she stared hard into my eyes, as if daring me to repeat a word of what she was going to say next:

'Dad didn't buy it for me,' she said. 'It's not expensive.'

I felt puzzled. Why was she crying then?

'It's not expensive,' she said, 'but it is valuable. To me. It's valuable to me ... '

I looked at my trainers. One lace had snapped off and the other had been trailing in mud and lake water. I glanced across at Lindy's shoes – bright white, brand new Nikes. As I watched a snot bubble fell from her nose onto the toe of one of them. She didn't even notice.

'The necklace is really special because it belonged to my gran,' Lindy sighed. 'She gave it to me before she died. I loved my gran. Whenever I wear it, it reminds me of her ... of all the lovely ...' she started to cry again.

'Oh,' I said. 'Where did you lose it?'

The claws came out in a flash. 'Well if I knew that it wouldn't be lost, would it?' she snapped.

'I meant,' I put on my most patient voice, like when I try to explain the off-side rule in soccer to Ella, 'did you lose it here in the reserve?'

'Yes,' she sniffed. 'I had it on when I got here with my sisters, but they left to look in the gift shop. I tried to catch up with them, but then I noticed that it's gone.'

'I'm sure they'll help you find it,' I said doubtfully. Dylan, Harvey, Hannah and Ella would be getting worried about where I was.

'They won't. They love it when I get into trouble with Mum and Dad, they say that I'm their favourite,' she said, more to herself than me. 'It's not true. It's just that I'm the youngest so Daddy always makes them look after me when we go out. Cara and Josie spend all their time trying to lose me. They hate me.'

'I'm sure they don't.'

'They HATE me!' she cried. 'Mummy and Daddy can't be bothered. The only one who liked me at all was Gran and now I've lost her necklace.'

The tears started falling again. I gulped and reached my arm out to Lindy, but she backed away from me.

'Just go,' she said. 'Go and upload your entry. I know how much you want to win those passes. My sisters wouldn't help me today so I'm out of the competition anyway. You could still win. Go!'

I stood up to go. Lindy was right. We could still win. I needed to go. If Team Trixie's photo was one of the first uploads, we would win the tickets. I would finally get to experience Planet Thrill.

I looked at Lindy, clutching onto her knotted up tissue. She'd be OK. She'd find the necklace and then she could get a VIP ticket anyway. Couldn't she? I thought back to what she'd just said. Maybe everything at home wasn't quite as fabulous as she always made out. Her sisters certainly didn't seem very nice.

I closed my eyes and screwed up my face. When I opened them Lindy was looking straight back at me.

'I do want to win,' I said. 'But not like this. We'll help you find your necklace.'

When I finally made it up to the top of Heron Hill with Lindy Lawson it tow, the others gawped at us like we were a pair of little green men from outer space.

Hannah raised one eyebrow. 'Care to explain?'

'Have you done it?' I asked, ignoring the question. 'The upload?'

'No!' said Dylan. 'We didn't have your mum's password to log into the Planet Thrill website. We've been waiting for you. I thought you were going to the bathroom.'

Ella shifted awkwardly from foot to foot.

Harvey pointed at Lindy. 'What's going on then, Jen?'

'Something came up,' I said. 'Look. Lindy's lost her gran's necklace. It's really precious. We need to help her find it.'

The thing about my friends is that they've always got my back. They will stick their necks out even when they're not quite sure what we're doing, or if I've made a crazy decision – like suddenly deciding to help out a ten-year-old nightmare who has been ruining our lives since we can remember. When I need my friends they always step up. That is the best feeling.

Once they knew what needed to be done, we all legged it back down the hill. Hannah and the others spread out across the park, roping in groups of families, kids and treasure hunters to help. I raced back to reception and asked the rangers to put an announcement out on the speakers.

'Look what I've done,' said Ella, when I had made it all the way down to the lake again, panting to get my breath back. She'd messaged her mum and asked her to put an alert out on social media explaining about Lindy's lost necklace.

We dived into bushes, scrabbled across meadows and crawled through undergrowth, scouring every soggy centimetre of the reserve. Just before it was time to call it quits I found myself on the far side of the lake with Trixie, near the place where Lindy had fallen out with her sisters.

It was getting cold now. Soon there would not be enough light to stay out. Trixie was already tugging me in the other direction, thinking about her dinner.

Then, suddenly I saw it, a glint of gold. There was Lindy's beautiful chain, twinkling and glittering from a tree branch.

She was super-grateful. No, really she was. She almost hugged me ... *almost*. But then the idea was too much so she stepped back and smiled at me instead. Her words at least seemed to come from the heart:

'Oh, I can't believe it! You found it. Thank you, Jenny. And your puppy, too! I bet she sniffed it out, didn't she?'

'Well actually it was me this time, I ... '

'Clever pup, so cute,' gushed Lindy. 'Well done, you little poochie-woochie-woo.' She ruffled Trixie's ears up and down

– a bit hard, really. She's not keen on having her ears rubbed, but she put up with it just this once.

'I'm glad that's sorted,' I said brightly. 'Now we can go and upload our ... '

But Lindy's interest in me and my life had vanished. She gave Trixie a last pat on the head, waved at the others and then, necklace in hand, skipped off to find her sisters.

It was too late now to go back to Heron Hill. The reserve was closing and it was too dark anyway. It would have to wait 'til we got back to mine.

'Why don't you just send the photo to your Mum,' suggested Hannah.

'OK.' I attached the picture to

a text message, but I wasn't sure it had sent.

It took an age to bike home. Mum and Dad were sat waiting on the doorstep for us, each holding a mug of tea. They had been tracking us on Mum's phone.

'Well done, guys!' Dad said.

I jumped off my bike and tore up the lawn. 'Did you get the message?' I asked. 'Did you upload the picture to the Planet Thrill site?'

'Oh Jen,' Mum said, giving me a hug. 'I have uploaded it, but the site was down for ages. I guess lots of people were uploading at the same. I got it up there eventually, but... ' She paused, not wanting to break the spell. 'The winners have been announced, Jenny. Team Trixie wasn't among the first. I'm afraid you were just too late.'

•   •   •

Consolation Cake

Is there anything more depressing than wiping off face paint? It's so much fun to see it go on, watching layer upon layer build up, decorating your smile with rainbow colours. But wiping it off, well that's just torture.

'Sit still,' Ella said, rubbing my black nose with a wet wipe. I stared at myself in the mirror. Behind me I could see Harvey poking at the bits

Hannah had missed. Dylan caught my eye in the mirror and followed my gaze to the corner of the room. My waste bin was overflowing with paint-streaked wipes and tissues and the crumpled up animation ideas I'd torn down as soon as we'd got up here.

'A graveyard of dreams,' he said heavily.

'What?' I muttered.

'The bin. It's a metaphor for our dreams of winning the Planet Thrill tickets. Dreams that have now been totally trashed.'

'Thanks for that, D!' said Hannah. 'Just what we need right now.'

He was right though. Our dreams had been well and truly dumped in the trash.

'We were so close,' sighed Ella.

'If it wasn't for ... ' She stopped mid-sentence.

'For helping someone out?' I said. 'For being kind and putting someone else's needs first?'

'I know you're right,' insisted Ella. 'Of course I'm glad we helped Lindy find her necklace, it's just ... '

'You wish we'd been able to do that *and* upload our finder's clip in time to win?' Harvey finished. 'Me too, Ella.'

'Me three,' smiled Hannah.

I turned to face them all. My friends. Tired, disappointed and smeary.

'It *is* gutting,' I said, 'but we had fun along the way, didn't we?'

They nodded.

'And we've aced the animation project for Coding Club,' I reminded them. 'We could use any one of those Team Trixie clips and Miss Pearson would think it was the best thing ever.'

'Right,' agreed Hannah. 'We could even splice them all together somehow and make a longer sequence. That would be cool.'

We carried on scrubbing out our faces for ages before anyone spoke.

'I wonder what Lindy's up to now?' Ella said.

'Probably lying in her massive four-poster bed, wearing her gold necklace and eating grapes peeled by Mummy and Daddy,' Hannah offered.

I bit my lip. After our conversation this afternoon I was pretty sure that was not how Lindy Lawson would be spending her evening, but I had promised to not to say anything.

'How long 'til your Mum gets here?' I asked Hannah.

'She said half an hour, but she might be later. She's dropping Dylan and Harvey home too.'

'I've got about ten minutes,' piped up Ella. 'Dad said I could only stay to get the face paint off. He's settling Robbie.'

'Let's go downstairs, then,' I said, trying to make the best of it. 'Dad said that he'd make us some hot chocolate.'

We ditched the rest of the wipes and headed downstairs. Dad winked at us when we came in, then pointed to the stools lined up along the kitchen counter. Five mugs had been set out in a row. He was already frothing up the milk for our drinks.

'Thanks Mr Many,' said Dylan flatly. 'Don't suppose I could have a bowl of Star Flakes with that? Looks like those vouchers are the only way we're going to get near Planet Thrill.'

'Why don't you have a night off tonight? suggested Dad.

'Only one hundred and seventeen more packets to go,' I muttered. 'We can wait.'

Dad didn't answer. Instead he lifted the cover off a glass cake stand.

'What's that?'

'I know it won't entirely make up for what happened,' said Dad, 'and I'm sure your parents won't thank me for filling you with this much sugar before bed, but I made this for the team.'

It was a Trixie Truffle cake. Dad

is a legend at icing, but this time he'd really outdone himself. The expression was exactly Trixie – her little pink tongue was lolling out and he'd even somehow managed to make the buttercream look like curly fur.

'I guess it's a *consolation* rather than a celebration cake now,' he told us, 'but it'll still taste delicious.'

I gave him the tightest hug ever, then he passed each of us a frothy mug of hot chocolate and a way too big slice of Trixie Truffle cake.

'Where's Mum?' I asked between mouthfuls.

'Not sure. Must be in her office. She was checking her phone, so maybe she had a work email to answer.'

'JENNY!'

After an ear-wincing shriek and a clatter of shoes on the hall floor Mum burst into the kitchen in a very un-Mum-like hurry.

We all stared at her. Her face was flushed and she was holding out her phone. I honestly thought someone had died.

'Don't look so worried,' she said. 'It's nothing bad. Thank goodness you kids are all still here. I've got something to show you!'

Mum held out the phone. She must have been looking at the Instagram account for Planet Thrill. Our Trixie animation uploads were on there – plus 10,546 comments! Mum tapped the screen and scrolled down:

Awesome!
Super cute.
This is my fave upload from the whole competition.
Who did this? It's great.

My mouth fell wide open. Over 10,000 comments raving about our animation? Mum clicked off the Planet Thrill account and moved onto 'Trending Now'. At the top of the list of popular threads was #PlanetThrillDog. Mum passed the phone to Dylan then Harvey, then Ella, and finally me and Hannah. There were thousands and thousands more comments and reposts of our uploads. I even spotted memes based on our animations! It was unbelievable.

'Everyone loves Trixie!' yelled Dylan.

'It would seem so,' agreed Mum. 'Everyone's talking about the kids with the cool dog. And look, someone has linked it back to our @Fluffadoodle account and now that's trending too!'

I blinked at the screen. Before life had been taken up with the treasure quest we'd had around 300 followers. Now the screen showed 15,000 and the digits were climbing every time we hit refresh.

'This is huge!' I said, 'MEGA! Wait 'til we show our animations at school! Everyone will freak when they realise that this is all down to us.'

'Team Trixie forever!' Hannah said, raising her mug.

'Team Trixie forever!' we echoed.

We hadn't won the tickets to Planet Thrill, but we sure could code.

We were just waving Ella up the drive when it happened. Dylan, Harvey and Hannah were putting their shoes on, ready to go home. Then the phone rang.

'Uh-huh,' we heard Dad say. 'Really? Well that's great. I'm sure they'd love to. Of course. Let's speak more tomorrow.'

There was a click as the receiver went down. Dad walked back into the hall and sat down on the step.

'Now listen, chaps,' he said. 'That was someone from Planet Thrill. They're not pleased with the response your upload is getting from the general public.'

We gazed up at him. What had we done wrong? We had uploaded an animated clip, rather than photos like everyone else. Maybe we'd caused their site to glitch ... or something worse. My stomach did a worried forward roll. Dylan gawped at Harvey. Ella ran back up the drive. Hannah just stared at the floor.

'No,' Dad continued. 'They're certainly not pleased.'

My stomach did a back flip and then a somersault. Nobody spoke.

'Because they are absolutely blooming delighted!'

He let that sink in for a little while. My mum and I always say Dad ought to be on the stage.

'The competition organisers are so happy with the response to your uploads, they've invited you all to come and officially open the park. Hope you're all free two weeks on Friday.'

I let out a scream of delight. Ella and Harvey danced about like a pair of over-excited baboons. Hannah grabbed Dylan and began to kiss his cheeks really hard. His neck went very red, but he didn't seem to mind.

'There is one condition though,' said Dad.

'What?' we all cried at once. 'What condition? We'll do anything!'

'You bring the star guest along. The real Trixie dog!'

And then it was pandemonium. No one minded that Trixie was barking like a lunatic, that we'd eaten half a kilo of icing each, that we still had faces showing more paint than skin or even that we were still up at almost eleven pm on a Sunday night.

Sometimes you've just got to do what you've got to do.

• • •

As Good as Gold

So that's it really, the whole story. I told you it was a big adventure! The two weeks leading up to the park opening whooshed past in a blur. Everyone at school knew what we had been up to. We were like celebrities in the playground, although in class it was just the same getting told off and having homework and trying to stop Emily 'borrowing' rubbers from my pencil case without asking.

People wanted to know all sorts of stuff. Whether I could sneak Trixie into school so they could pet her (NO), whether Ella could do puppy face-paints for birthday parties (YES), and whether it was true that a full-length *Trixie Dog* feature film was coming out at the cinema soon (NO, but wouldn't that be awesome?).

As soon as I could I went by myself to say thank you to Miss Pearson. It was the stuff we had learnt in Coding Club that made our Team Trixie uploads stand out from all those thousands of entries. I couldn't wait to show her what we'd come up with.

'This is amazing Jenny!' she said, clapping her hands together. 'I'm so impressed. Did you do this by yourself?'

'Of course not,' I said. 'I did it with my friends.'

Mrs Pearson turned out to be so bowled over by our work that she wanted to stretch us even further. 'How about one more clip – to celebrate your appearance on launch day?' she suggested.

'Yeah!' I said. 'We could show Trixie at the park – on a rollercoaster!'

'Great idea,' she said. 'Get your gang to Coding Club tonight and we'll start work straight away.

Within a week we had something OUT OF THIS WORLD ready to upload on @Fluffadoodle. Our 20,000 followers just loved it! The Planet Thrill PR guy even phoned to thank us for all the extra clicks to their site from ours.

'We can't wait to see you on Friday,' he said. 'Make sure you come to the VIP entrance.'

Friday was the slowest day at school EVER. Somehow I got through the day, even though we had a maths test and then in art someone clumsy who will remain nameless (Dylan Wilkins) accidentally spilled water all over my painting.

As we lined up in the cloakroom ready for hometime I caught Lindy looking at me. I smiled. She didn't smile back, but she did come over.

'I've still got the necklace,' she said, burrowing her fingers inside her shirt collar and hooking out the locket.

I nodded. 'Good.'

'You doing that theme park thing this evening?' she asked.

'Yeah. Tonight's the big night.'

'Right.'

Lindy looked awkward, but she didn't move. I was just about to pick up my backpack and go when she caught hold of my arm.

'I just wanted to say that your Trixie rollercoaster clip ... it's really good.'

'Thanks,' I said. 'Well, I guess I'll see you tonight at the opening.'

The door to the classroom banged. Jane poked her head round expectantly and Lindy's face hardened at once. Her voice went up a few notches. 'No, I won't be there,' she scowled. 'My tickets are for next week when all the rush dies down. That's when it's more *exclusive*.'

'Ah,' I said. 'OK. See you then.' I

put on my backpack then bent down to retie my laces. By the time I stood up, Lindy and Jane had disappeared.

It's difficult to describe how unutterably brilliant that evening was. We really did get to open Planet Thrill – we even got to cut a big red ribbon with massive scissors. I did the snipping while Dylan, Ella, Harvey and Hannah waited on the podium holding Trixie's lead. When I finished, everybody cheered and she actually walked on her hind legs then did a flip, all on her own, without a treat. The crowd went wild for her. Well ... wouldn't you?

And then we got to be the very first people on every ride. Each one was just as spectacular as I had imagined it would be, but the Golden Orbiter was the very best. I sat in the car next to Hannah, about a mile above the city, watching the twinkling lights and listening to the excited squeals and shrieks of all the other Thrill Seekers below.

'I may not have won the tickets,' I said, 'but I really did strike gold.'

Hannah threw back her head and laughed. I love watching her laugh. I love seeing all my friends having fun. They deserve it – I wouldn't be here without them. I threw my arm around Hannah's back and stretched over to wave at the carriage behind us. Ella, Harvey and Dylan were all scrunched up in a row, looking sparkly and happy.

'Hey Ella!' I called. 'You glad we're here?'

'Yeah!' she shouted back. 'But not as glad as Dylan.'

I raised my eyebrows. 'Why's that?'

Harvey was already in fits of giggles. Dylan gave him a silly wink before he piped up:

'Because now we've been to Planet Thrill I can finally stop eating Star Flakes!'

A Message to the Grown-ups.....

Jenny Many is a bold and exuberant ten-year old who loves cake, coding, the clarinet and her oh-so-cute canine, Trixie. Jenny is a fallible, yet hugely relatable hero. She falls down and picks herself back up, makes mistakes but always tries her best to put them right again. Through her 'many' friends and adventures, Jenny discovers the power of teamwork, respect and mutual support.

We created Jenny Many as an antidote to some of the biggest anxieties parents and our children face as we make our way through the modern world. How can we encourage our children to develop both a strong sense of self and empathy for others? How do we embrace technology in a positive way whilst still encouraging face-to-face communication and creativity? How can we allow our children the freedom to explore the world, but keep them safe every step of the way? How do we teach them to be global citizens – both one of many and one for many?

Our children are constantly being confronted with challenges that threaten to affect their wellbeing. How can they be accepted in their social group whilst forging their own path? Will making the right choice rather than taking the popular option see them ostracized? Is academic achievement really the only way to success?

We want to make a positive impact on the lives of children, helping them to begin to find the answers to some of these questions.